FLIGHT OF THE GREY GOOSE

FLIGHT OF THE GREY GOOSE

VICTOR CANNING

HEINEMANN
NEW WINDMILLS

Heinemann Educational Books Ltd
Halley Court, Jordan Hill, Oxford OX2 8EJ
OXFORD   LONDON   EDINBURGH
MADRID   ATHENS   BOLOGNA   PARIS
MELBOURNE   SYDNEY   AUCKLAND
IBADAN   NAIROBI   HARARE   GABORONE
SINGAPORE   TOKYO   PORTSMOUTH NH (USA)

ISBN 0 435 12199 5

92 93 94 95 15 14 13 12 11 10 9 8 7

Printed in England by Clays Ltd, St Ives plc

For Fiona with love

Contents

I

∽ Destination Unknown ∽

It was a fresh, sunny morning in July. Big puffballs
of cloud rolled lazily across the sky from the west. In
a lay-by at the side of the main road, a grey squirrel
was sitting on the edge of the rubbish bin, fastid-
iously nibbling at a stale piece of cake which it had
found.

A little farther down the road was a boy with not
many months to go before he reached the age of
sixteen. At his feet was a battered old suitcase. He
was tallish, fair-haired, and well built with a friendly,
squarish face – heavily freckled under his sun-tan – a
pressed-in smudge of a nose and a pair of angelic
blue eyes which, when he put on his special smile,
made him look as though butter wouldn't melt in his
mouth. From the cheerful grin on his face as he
waved to the traffic it would have been difficult to
believe that that morning early he had given the
police the slip for the second time in the last six
months. He was wanted by them for absconding
from an approved school. Although his friends called
him Smiler his real name was Samuel Miles. Actually
he preferred Samuel M., because that was what his
father called him. That, too, was what he called himself when he gave himself a good talking-to – which
he often did when he had some problem to face. And
on this sunny July morning Smiler really did have a
problem to face because by now the police forces of
Dorset, Wiltshire, Hampshire and a few other
counties were all on the lookout for him.

"Unless, Samuel M.," he told himself, "you pick up a lift soon and get out of this area some police car is going to come along and pick you up. And then, my lad, you'll be sunk for good and all."

It was at this moment that a long, high-cabbed white lorry came down the road towards him. Smiler gave it a wave and a cheery grin automatically. To his surprise the lorry pulled up slowly just beyond him. Smiler ran down the road to it.

The driver leaned over and opened the nearside cab door. He was a round-faced man of about forty with an old white cap perched on the back of his head, the peak pushed up at a sharp angle. He wore green overalls, had a broad smile on his face, and alongside him on the bench seat sat a largish black dog with a white patch on its chest and a large grin on its face.

The driver said, "Where you headin' for, son?"

Smiler said, "I dunno, exactly."

The driver chuckled. "Destination unknown. Good as any. Hop in. You're the second this morning."

Smiler swung his case and then himself up into the cab and closed the door. The lorry moved off down the road.

Smiler, who was polite by nature and by policy, said, "Thank you very much, sir."

The driver chuckled. It was a nice, friendly, happy sound. "Strictly 'gainst company rules. But all rules is made to be broken at times. You want to sit and brood over your worries or listen to the radio or talk? Take your choice. All the same to me."

Smiler said, "I don't mind talking, sir."

"Wise choice," said the driver. "Silence is golden but weighs heavy. The radio is full of woe – or pop

2

music which is worse. But talk is human and friendly. Also, don't call me 'sir'. I'm Bob Peach. Peachy my friends call me, but you stick to Mr. Bob till I tell you you've served your time which –" he winked "– could be anything from an hour to a hundred years 'cording to the way things go."

"Yes, Mr. Bob," said Smiler.

"Well then," said Bob Peach, "go ahead."

"Go ahead what?" asked Smiler.

"Go ahead and talk. That's your choice. You got to start. Only fair."

Smiler, a little unsure of Bob Peach, was silent for a moment and then said, "What did you mean that I'm the second this morning?"

Bob Peach nodded towards the dog which was sitting between them. "Him. Another 'Destination unknown'. Like you. Sittin' I was, havin' a bite of breakfast by the road, when up he walks, no collar, no name, free as air and cadges a bacon sandwich from me. Bit skinny, ain't he? But he'll fatten up. Hops in the cab with me, won't take 'Go home' for an answer. Probably because he ain't got one and here he is. Sitting like a lord and not a word to be got out of him."

Smiler took a good look at the dog. He knew quite a bit about dogs and liked them. This was a biggish dog, but in no way a pedigree one. There were touches of Alsatian and sheepdog about him. He was quite pleasant to look at but definitely very much a mixture. The dog looked at Smiler, panted a little with the warmth in the cab and let a long red tongue flop over the side of his mouth. Smiler scratched him behind the ears and the dog shut his brown eyes in ecstasy.

3

"He ought to have a name," said Smiler.

"If he's got one he won't tell. What do you reckon we should call him?"

"Rex?" suggested Smiler.

"Too grand. He ain't no aristocrat. He's a good, common, solid, mixed up all-dog dog. What's your name?"

"Samuel," said Smiler.

"Samuel what?"

"Samuel Miles," said Smiler and wondered why, in the circumstances, he was being so truthful – except that with someone like Bob Peach it wouldn't have seemed right not to be. Then, to avoid any further questions about himself, he went on quickly, "What do you think he should be called, Mr. Bob?"

Bob Peach, his eyes on the road ahead as he drove, said, "Bacon. I been thinkin' about it coming along. Things like names must be fitting always. And that's what brought us together. The smell of that bacon sandwich. What do you think of that?"

"I don't see why not," said Smiler. "I used to know a horse called that."

"Horse or dog, no matter," said Bob Peach. "It's a good name. Comes well off the tongue either in anger or love, and not going to be answered by any other riffraff of Fidos, Tims, or Rovers or what-have-yous. All right then, that's settled. Subject number one discussed and disposed of. What's the second item on the agenda?"

Smiler said, "It's your turn, isn't it, Mr. Bob, to start something?"

"So it is. Fair's fair. Well then, let me see. What about a few personal questions? You got a father and mother?"

"No mother, Mr. Bob. She died when I was a baby. But I got a father." Smiler said it proudly for he considered he had the best father in the world. He added, "He's in the merchant navy. A cook. He's away at sea right now."

"A sea-faring man. There's a life. Here today and gone tomorrow. Just like me. Long distance driving. Always something different coming up over the horizon. A great life if you've got a touch of the gypsy in you."

"What do you carry in this truck, Mr. Bob?" asked Smiler, who was rather keen to steer away from too much personal talk.

"Marine stores and equipment. From Southampton. Going to Bristol now. Then on to Birmingham and Liverpool and then back home again. Since you don't know where you want to go you can take your choice of any of 'em or some spot along the route."

Smiler, who had been born in Bristol and had a Sister Ethel who lived there still with her husband, Albert, wasn't too keen on Bristol. When his father was at sea he lived with them. Although he liked both of them Smiler wasn't too comfortable living with them. They were very fussy about the tidiness of their spick and span little house and grumbled because his hands were always marking the fresh paintwork. People, somehow, always seemed to be making a fuss about what he did. . . . Well, of some of the things. Like pinching a bottle of milk from a doorstep if he was thirsty, or nicking a book from a shop if he felt like reading. Though there had never been any call to send him to approved school because he just hadn't done what they had said he had done. The last thing in the world he would have done would have been to pinch an old lady's handbag with twenty pounds in it. Still, when his father got back he would settle all that. That was why, after exactly thirteen days' and four hours' residence in the approved school, Smiler had run away and had been managing on his own ever since. In the last few months Smiler had become very good at looking after himself.

He said, "I'm not keen on Bristol, Mr. Bob. Could I go to Liverpool?"

"Liverpool it is. Or any place in between that you might happen to fancy. Shan't get there until tomorrow. But you and Bacon can kip down in the cab tonight if that suits. All right?"

"Yes, thank you, Mr. Bob."

Bob Peach smiled to himself. He had two boys of his own, though they were much older than Smiler, and there was not much he had to learn about boys. He could tell a boy who was in trouble easily enough. And he could sense very quickly whether a boy was a bad or a good apple. This Samuel Miles was in some kind of trouble, but he was prepared to bet that he wasn't really a bad sort. But Bob Peach knew too that you had to take your time with boys in trouble. No good pressing them. If they wanted your help or advice they would ask for it in their own good time. Until then you just kept things going nice and easy and didn't ask any awkward questions.

So Bob Peach drove to Bristol and part of the time he and Smiler talked, and part of the time they listened to the radio or were just silent with their own thoughts. In between them sat Bacon, leaning against Smiler and settling down happily in friendly company in the way all dogs of good character and no fixed abode do. And every time that Smiler saw a police car parked ahead by the road, he would bend over and pretend to scratch his ankle, keeping his head well down until the car had been passed.

When they reached Bristol and Bob Peach drove the lorry into a yard to unload part of his stores, Smiler strolled out into the road and found a telephone booth. All Smiler possessed in the world was the thirty odd pounds he had saved up from the job he had worked at during the past few months, his battered old suitcase with a few clothes and odds and ends in it, and the clothes he stood up in; a rough blue shirt, a shabby green anorak and a pair of patched blue jeans. Being at large in Bristol made him uneasy. Some of his old school friends might spot him or – if he were dead unlucky – he might run into Sister Ethel or his Brother-in-Law Albert, so he was glad that there was a telephone booth just around the corner from the yard. He looked up the number of his father's shipping company in the directory and called it. Making his voice sound as rough and grownup as he could he asked when the *Kentucky Master* was due back in the country and at what port. He was told that at the moment she was scheduled for some time at the beginning of October at Greenock. After making this call Smiler contemplated ringing his Sister Ethel to tell her he was all right and she was not to worry – which he knew she would do anyway. But he decided against it. It would be better to write her a letter in a few days' time when he was well out of the Bristol area. Then he went back to the yard and sat waiting in the cab of the truck until Mr. Bob had been unloaded and was ready to move on. There was some trouble over the load which Mr. Bob was delivering, and it was some time before they moved off.

After leaving Bristol Bob Peach drove northwards through the green English countryside with Bacon and Smiler beside him. Now and again Bob would flash his lights or blow his horn to some passing lorry driver he knew. In the fields the cows grouped themselves under the broad shade of trees. Rooks gritting on the road ahead of them flew up as they approached and, in the clear air above, the swallows and swifts performed their aerobatics. They went through small country towns and large industrial towns and past farms and cottages. Most of the time, whatever they were talking about, Smiler was thinking that it was a long time to October and that he would have to get himself settled in somewhere safe and sound and find himself a job. His thirty pounds would not last for ever.

Once he said, "Where's Greenock, Mr. Bob?"

"Greenock. That's on the Clyde. Near Glasgow. Take a load up there sometimes. Why?"

"That's where my father's ship berths."

"Oh, want to get up there, do you?"

"Well, not just yet. Not till October."

"And what you goin' to do until then?"

"Get myself a job, I suppose. I don't like doin' nothing."

"Neither do I. Takes all the sap out of you."

For a moment Bob Peach considered pursuing enquiries about Samuel Miles, but decided against it. If the boy wanted help he would ask for it soon enough. He seemed a capable sort and able to look after himself.

At seven o'clock they stopped at a transport café

and had a meal and Smiler got a plate of scraps from the kitchen for Bacon. Some time later Bob Peach turned off the main highway on to a side road. Half a mile down the road was a large picnic area on the edge of a wood. Bob Peach pulled into this.

He said, "Can't take staying in transport lodgings in the summer. Kip out in the open. Saves money and it's healthier. You and Bacon can have the cab, I'll sleep in the back. Now then, why don't you and Bacon take a stroll before turning in? I'm going to sit and read me paper over a bottle of beer." He pulled from his pocket the evening paper and a bottle of beer which he had bought at the transport café.

Smiler and Bacon jumped down from the cab and moved off into the trees. Although Smiler had been born and lived nearly all his life in Bristol he had in the last few months become very much of a country boy and now knew that, next to shipping off to sea like his father, he would prefer always to live and work in the country. He went happily through the trees with Bacon at his heels.

Behind him Bob Peach took a swig at his bottle of beer and shook open the evening paper. His eyes rounded with surprise. "Cor, luv a duck!" he said.

There, staring at him from the centre of a column on the front page, was a head and shoulders picture of Samuel Miles. Not a good photograph and one taken eighteen months before. But it was unmistakably Samuel Miles. The caption at the head of the column read – COUNTRYWIDE SEARCH FOR RUNAWAY BOY. Even as he began to read the account the thought went swiftly through Bob Peach's mind that half-a-dozen drivers had been reading the evening paper in the transport café. In fact, now he thought of it, one or two had given Samuel Miles an odd look as they had gone out. It would be a miracle if no one had recognized that broad, snub-nosed face, the thick freckles and the fair hair.

*　　*　　*

Some way in the wood, sitting by the side of a small lake with Bacon close to him, Smiler was eyeing the water. There wouldn't be any trout in it, he thought, but it looked good chub and carp water. Maybe some tench. A mallard duck moved along the fringe of reeds and bullrushes with a little flotilla of duck-lings following in line astern. A swallow dipped to the lake surface and made a ring like a rising fish. Life in the streets of Bristol had made his eyes sharp, but life in the Wiltshire countryside in the past months had made them even sharper. In the country you had to be all eyes and ears. Somewhere in the trees on the far bank a wood pigeon was cooing. A hatch of flies moved ceaselessly up and down in their mating dance over the reeds and he caught the flick of a waterhen's white scut under some overhanging branches. He thought of the times his father had taken him to places like this fishing, and also of his recent friend Joe Ringer who had taught him to poach trout and anything else that was going with the best of them. October was a long way ahead. A very long way. And Greenock was in Scotland. He knew nothing about Scotland except that up there they ate haggis and made whisky and wore kilts. His father was fond of a glass of whisky now and then. October. Scotland. He gave a sigh and shook his head. They were both a long way off. Funny look that chap in the transport kitchen had given him when he went to get the scraps for Bacon. Almost as though he knew him. Perhaps the police had put something on the radio about him. He remembered the last time he had escaped from the police when they were taking him back to approved school. Then, he had gone into hiding, kept right out of sight. "You was being hunted then, Samuel M.," he told himself, "and you acted sensible. But now . . . Blimey, you really haven't been very sensible. Staying right out in the open, riding the roads with Mr. Bob, giving everyone a chance to see you."

Bacon came back from foraging around the lakeside and thrust a wet muzzle against his ear. Smiler got up and began to go slowly back to Mr. Bob and the truck. He had made a quick decision. He would sleep the night in the truck, but early in the morning he would be up and away before Mr. Bob was awake. Mr. Bob was nice but there was nothing he could do if the police or anyone else spotted him. Yes, that's what he would do. Take off and keep clear of roads and towns until the hunt for him had cooled off a bit. After that he could look for a job of some kind. Thank goodness, too, the weather was good. He could sleep rough in the open for weeks yet if he had to.

He moved through the trees, away up the slope from the lake. A jay scolded him from the shelter of a hawthorn bush. A grey squirrel ran up the side of an oak trunk and somewhere, high up in one of the trees, a thrush began to sing. For a moment Smiler felt very sad. He liked company, and he liked Mr. Bob. He liked being settled and having a job and knowing that he only had to wait out time till his father got back and sorted out the approved school mix-up. Perhaps, he thought, he'd risk riding just a bit farther with Mr. Bob.

He reached the top of the small rise and began to move down towards the picnic area and Mr. Bob's truck, Bacon at his heels. Through the trees he could glimpse part of the white side of the truck. Then, as he drew nearer, he saw that a car was drawn up behind the truck and he heard the sound of men's voices. At this moment a man passed by the car, and the sight of him was enough to send Smiler diving for cover behind a bush. It was a police patrolman.

Smiler worked his way round to the other side of the bush and got a clearer view of the picnic area. What he saw made him give a quiet groan and his heart thump fast.

Drawn up by the truck was a police car. The blue light on its roof was still flashing. Standing by the car were two patrolmen and Mr. Bob. Mr. Bob had a newspaper in his hand and one of the policemen was pointing to something in it. The other policeman went quickly back to the police car and Smiler saw him pick up the hand microphone and begin to speak over the radio.

Smiler didn't wait for any more. He was bright enough to guess what could have happened. Mr. Bob had bought the evening paper in the transport café where the chap in the kitchen there had given him an odd look. "Samuel M.," he told himself, "if you want to keep out of trouble, this is no place for you."

He crouched down and moved away into the trees, taking all the cover he could. When he reached the top of the rise above the lake and was well out of sight, he straightened up and began to run. He found a grass-covered ride cut through the wood and jogged down it at a steady pace. It was then for the first time that he realized that Bacon was with him still, keeping close to his side, loping easily along, his red tongue flopping out of his mouth.

* * *

Two hours later the policemen, after having made a close search of the nearby woods for Smiler and Bacon, returned to Bob Peach.

"He must have come back and spotted us," said one of the policemen. "Took off again. Why won't a boy in trouble realize that you don't get anywhere by running away?"

Bob Peach gave a small grin and said, "If you really want to know, I'll tell you. Because he's a boy, and all boys is young animals with an instinct to keep away from you boys in blue. Here –" he reached inside the cab and pulled out Smiler's battered case "– you'd better have this. Stuffed full of the crown jewels it probably is."

The policeman gave him a sour look and took the case.

The other policeman said, "What was this dog like he had with him?"

Bob Peach screwed up his face for a moment in thought and then said, "Well, I'd say it was kind of smallish. Half-terrier, half-corgi. All white, except for one brown ear. You could recognize it a mile off 'cause it runs with a kind of limp." He paused, and then added, "The left ear – that's the brown one. I know you chaps like all details to be exact."

2

∽ The Professor Takes a Hand
— and More ∽

For two days Smiler and Bacon avoided civilization
as much as they could. If they had to cross a road
they waited until it was more or less clear and
crossed quickly. When Smiler had to buy food
and drink he would slip into a small village store and
then be gone like a shadow. He had found an old
sack and some binder twine and made himself a
small haversack to carry provisions. He washed the
sack and his only shirt by a stream and dried them in
the sun. He bought himself a cap in a country shop
to cover his fair hair and he made a collar and a lead
from the binder twine for Bacon. But there was little
need for the lead because Bacon kept faithfully to
his heels and – somebody in the past had well-
trained Bacon – if Smiler told him to sit and mind his
haversack, Bacon would sit and guard it until he
returned.

Right from the start Smiler established what he
considered was the safest routine. Once the sun was
well up they stopped travelling and found a place to
hide and rest. The first night they slept on piles of
pulled green bracken in a little woodland dell five
miles from Mr. Bob's truck. As he lay there Smiler
looked up and picked out the Big Bear and then the
North Star. From his father he knew most of the
principal stars and he had already decided to head
northwards. They were up before dawn and, steering

now by the sun, kept going until almost mid-day when they found a place to rest until the afternoon was almost worn away.

The second night they found a stack of fresh cut hay, burrowed into it, and slept warm and comfortable with the sweet smell of new mown grass in their nostrils. Between them they ate meat pies, sausage rolls, corned beef, tinned sardines, biscuits, buns, apples, oranges and once – as a treat for Smiler – a small bottle of pickled onions. They drank spring and river water with now and then – for Smiler – a bottle of beer or a can of shandy or Coca-Cola. And once Smiler bought half-a-dozen brown eggs from a cottage and a new loaf from a village store. He made a fire and boiled the eggs hard in an old tin. He and Bacon finished the lot between them for supper with a can of salmon. Bacon showed no signs of distress, but Smiler was awake half the night with a violent stomach ache.

They went north steadily if slowly and erratically, and Smiler had no idea where he was. The names of the villages meant nothing to him. Sometime, he decided, he must buy a map so that he could find Greenock on it. Thinking things over he had come to the decision that if his father was going to berth at Greenock in October, then there was no reason why he shouldn't go to Scotland as soon as he could. England was all right but the police here knew all about him and had long memories and sharp eyes. Up in Scotland probably no one knew about him. He'd heard, too, that it was a wild sort of country of mountains and lochs and rivers with plenty of room for a person to find a niche for himself without risk of meeting a policeman at every turn of the road.

On their fourth day at large, as they were travelling after their afternoon rest, it began to rain in a steady downpour. They were moving across a wide stretch of orchard country, the trees globed with green, unripened apples. Within five minutes the two were as wet as fishes and far more uncomfortable. With Bacon at his heels, long bushy tail bedraggled and lowered to a half-mast position, Smiler ploughed on looking for some shelter. The trees gave no cover. They just seemed to drip more water as well as rain on them. There wasn't a tractor shed or a barn in sight without going near a farmhouse. After two hours of wet and miserable walking they came out on to a main road. In the fading light Smiler saw, stacked just off the road, a pile of large section concrete pipes which had been unloaded there in preparation for some drainage works. A few cars were zipping up and down the road, their lights on and their tires hissing on the wet surface.

Smiler surveyed the pipe sections. Bacon at his side gave himself a shake and sprayed water from his coat. "Samuel M.," said Smiler, "any port in a storm and beggars can't be choosers."

He crawled into the cover of one of the pipes. Bacon went with him and drew close to him so that Smiler could feel the dog shiver now and then. Smiler sat there and watched the occasional car go by. All the food he had left in his sodden sack was a sliced loaf and a piece of cheese. He pulled them out. The loaf slices were sodden with rain. Smiler broke the cheese in half and wrapped two limp, doughy, soggy slices of bread round each half. He gave one to Bacon who ate it ravenously. He ate the other himself and tried to pretend that it was a delicious cheese roll. A cold draught blew through the pipe and the concrete was hard on his bottom, elbows and shoulders as he tried to make himself comfortable. It was, he knew, going to be a long and uncomfortable night.

To cheer himself up, he began to think of his father. Living in Bristol with his Sister Ethel and her Albert was all right, but nothing like as good as the times when his father was ashore and they lived together in lodgings, went on fishing expeditions and to football matches. Where was his father now, he wondered? Berthed in some foreign port? A warm, tropical night all around and palms rustling in the soft breeze and fireflies flitting about their tops. Probably he'd be sitting on deck in the cool after the heat of the galley and giving the other lads a song. A great singer was his father and he, Smiler, knew all his songs. Perhaps, he thought, if he gave himself a song, pretended that he was warm and comfortable, it would help. He began to sing one of his father's favourites –

> *There were two ravens that sat on a tree*
> *And they were black as they could be;*
> *And one of them I heard him say –*
> *Oh where shall we go to dine today?*
> *Shall we go down to the salt, salt sea –*
> *Or shall we go dine by the green-wood tree?*
> *Shall we go down to the salt, salt sea –*
> *Or shall we go dine by the green-wood tree?*

But as he finished the first verse, Bacon raised himself on his forefeet, lifted his head up and began to howl like a wolf. He made so much noise that Smiler had to stop singing in case someone heard them both. There was nothing for it but to try and get some sleep, so Smiler curled himself up and, using Bacon as a damp pillow, shut his eyes and wooed sleep. It was a long time coming, but when it did he slept soundly.

Smiler woke the next morning just as the sun was coming up. The rain had gone. Early morning traffic was beginning to move up and down the road. Stiffly, he and Bacon emerged from their pipe and went back over the hedge to get away from the road. Both of them were damp, bedraggled and hungry. They ploughed through the wet long grass of a meadow, the grass starred with tall ox-daisies and creamy spikes of meadowsweet above which the bees were already long busy. The top of the meadow was bounded by a small, fast-running stream. Smiler took a look at the sun and saw that the stream was running from the north to the south, so he began to move upstream with Bacon at his heels.

After about a hundred yards Smiler suddenly stopped and raised his head and sniffed. He sniffed two or three times and slowly his mouth began to water. He looked down at Bacon and said, "Bacon, my lad – if there's one morning smell that you can't mistake it's eggs and bacon frying."

Slowly the two moved cautiously upstream, following the delicious smell. They came to a small clump of willows growing at the stream side and went into them. The smell grew stronger. In the middle of the clump, close to the stream's edge, they saw a large sheet of black plastic material which had been tied in a canopy between four trees with the loose ends pegged down on three sides to make a snug shelter. The opening faced away from them.

Over the top of the sheeting a thin, blue curl of wood smoke showed and the smell of cooking was very pungent and appetizing.

With Bacon close to his heels Smiler moved around the side of the shelter. Just in front of it was a small fire, burning in a neat fireplace made from stones taken from the stream. On the fire was a large frying-pan which held four rashers of bacon, two eggs and a sausage, all sizzling gently away. It was a sight which made Smiler's midriff ache. Sitting just outside the tent affair on a small canvas folding stool was a man with a long twig in his hand with which he was turning the sausage and bacon as they cooked.

He looked up at Smiler without surprise. Then he looked at Bacon. And then he looked back at Smiler and slowly winked.

Smiler, anxious to establish good relations, said politely, "Good morning, sir."

The man said, "Good morning, boy." He looked Smiler up and down again and it was the kind of look that missed nothing. Then he said, "A good morning after a bad night. How did you and your companion, *canis mongrelis*, make out?"

"Not very well, sir," said Smiler. "We slept in a drainpipe by the road back there."

The man nodded. "In my time I have done the same, but it is not to be recommended. Man was not framed to sleep on the arc of a circle. It is a question of the relative inflexibility of the human spine. I presume that it was the aroma of a traditional English breakfast that brought you this way?"

"We're both pretty hungry, sir. That's if you've got enough to spare. I could pay for it. I've got some money and –"

The man raised a warning hand. "Please, boy – do not mention money. Friendship and shared adversity are the only coinage recognized by true gentlemen of the road. Would I be right in putting you at two eggs and three rashers – plus a sausage? And for your faithful hound I have an old ham bone somewhere in my gear and he can have the pleasure of licking the frying-pan clean later."

"Gosh!" said Smiler. "That would be jolly super – if you can spare it."

"Say no more."

The man turned, reached back into his shelter, and dragged out a battered old perambulator with a tatty folded hood and began to ferret in it for provisions. In no time at all he had found eggs, bacon and sausage and they were in the frying-pan. The ham bone was unwrapped from an old newspaper and handed to Bacon. Then from the battered pram the man pulled out another folding canvas stool and handed it to Smiler saying, "Rest your juvenile posterior on that."

Smiler opened up the stool, sat down, and watched the man as he now began to give serious application to the cooking of an extra breakfast.

He was a funny-looking old boy, thought Smiler. He had long black hair to his shoulders and a straggling black beard. His face was brown and furrowed with wrinkles. Above a nobly beaked nose his eyes were as bright as a hedge-sparrow's eggs. Smiler, who wasn't much good at guessing ages, felt he must be much older than his father. For clothes, starting at the top, he wore a bowler hat whose blackness had a nice green shine like verdigris on copper, and his jacket was made of green and brown tweed and was patched and torn. His trousers were of blue denim and tucked into a pair of green gum boots. Underneath his open jacket he wore a red T-shirt on the front of which was a printed head of a man with long flowing hair and the word – Beethoven – under it.

The man looked up from his cooking and asked, "And what would your name be, boy?"

For a moment Smiler hesitated. Then he decided that this man didn't look the kind who would read the newspapers much or listen to the radio, so he decided to tell the truth.

"Samuel Miles, sir. Most people call me Smiler. But I don't care for it much."

"Neither do I since I don't care for half-cooked puns anymore than I do for half-cooked buns. I shall call you Samuel. And your four-legged friend?"

"That's Bacon."

"A good name. Of course, after the great philosopher and not the comestible of that ilk." Then seeing the baffled look on Smiler's face, he went on, "Never mind. Allow me to introduce myself. I am Professor Roscoe Bertram Crimples. That, of course, is my true name. I have others which necessity from time to time makes it desirable to employ. But then, as a gentleman of the road yourself, you, no doubt, understand that perfectly well."

"Yes, of course, sir . . . I mean, Professor," said Smiler.

"Capital, Samuel. We who live outside society must be allowed our little stratagems."

"What are you a Professor of?" asked Smiler.

The Professor reached back into the pram for two plates and cutlery and said over his shoulder, "I am a Professor of all the Ologies. You name one and I am a Professor of it." He turned and began to dish the breakfast from the frying-pan with a knife and fork. The sight and smell made Smiler's stomach feel hollow.

"Name an Ology," said the Professor severely.

A bit stumped for the moment, all his eyes and attention on the coming breakfast, Smiler searched around in his mind desperately and finally said, "What about Geology?"

"A fine subject. One of the oldest. *Granite is hard and sandstone is soft, but Time's withering hand turns all to dust.* I am, you see, also a bit of a poet – although the rhyme is bad which is due to the early hour of the day. Now let us eat while the water boils for our coffee."

He handed Smiler his plate and knife and fork, put an old tin can full of water into the embers of the fire, and then began to attack his own breakfast.

The two of them tucked into their breakfast while, a little way to the side, Bacon cracked and gnawed at the last of his bone. A bluetit came and sat on a branch above the canopy, scolded them, and then flew down to investigate a slip of bacon rind that Smiler tossed into the bushes for it. The stream ran behind them, making a pleasant musical sound, and the morning sun slid higher and bathed them with its warmth. It was one of the best breakfasts Smiler could remember and it was crowned by the Professor's coffee which was strong and laced with liberal dollops of sweet condensed milk.

Over his coffee, the Professor produced a small cheroot from the inside pocket of his jacket and lit it. He tipped his bowler hat back, blew a cloud of blue smoke, and contemplated Smiler. After a few moments he said, "Well, Samuel, state your problem."

A little guarded, Smiler said, "Problem, Professor? What problem?"

The Professor shook his head. "All mankind has problems. And that includes boys. Wandering about the country with a dog with a bit of string for a collar, carrying an old sack for luggage, spending a night in a concrete pipe – I don't have to be a Professor of Sociology to know you must have a problem. *Adrift on the troubled sea of life – victim of, who knows, what strife.* The metre's bad but the rhyme is good. I'll do better later in the day. So what's your problem?"

Smiler, who liked the man, still felt that he ought to be cautious.

He said, "It's a bit private, Professor."

"All problems are, more or less. But since I'm a Professor of Problemology, too, you can tell me. Troubles dealt with in the strictest confidence. No charge. But since you're not quite sure how to go about it, let's see if we can tackle it diplomatically. You're in trouble?"

"Yes, Professor."

"On the run?"

"Yes, Professor."

"Guilty or not guilty?"

"Of what, Professor?"

"Of what you're running away from, of course."

"No, I'm not. It was all a mistake and –"

"Hold it!" The Professor cut him off. "Not so fast. No need for details. I know truth when I hear it. Running away and not guilty. Good. Running where to?"

"Scotland, Professor."

"A fine country – though I never cared for it. The cooking is terrible. And why Scotland?"

" 'Cos my father's ship berths up there in October and I got to meet him so that he can sort things out for me."

"Splendid. He sounds like a good father. But Scotland's a long way off and so is October. Walking easily you could do it in a month."

"I want to get up there as soon as I can."

"Why?"

"Because – like I said – I'm on the run and the police down here –"

"– are keeping their sharp official little eyes open for you? Is that it?"

"Yes, Professor."

"The solution is simple. You've got money?"

"Yes, Professor."

"How much?"

"Twenty odd pounds."

"Then take a train."

Smiler shook his head. "I couldn't do that, Professor. I'd have to show myself at a station in some town. There's always police at stations. And on the train, too, there'd be people and the guard and ticket collector."

"Spare me the passenger list," said the Professor. "There are different ways of taking trains. Would you consider three pounds too expensive for a place on a train with no need for stations or meeting passengers and police?"

"Could you fix that, Professor?"

"Why not? I'm also a Professor of Fixology – for them that I like."

"Would you for me, Professor?"

"*Consider it a settled deal, No need for contract or big red seal.* Better. But still not of the highest order."

The Professor stood up and put the frying-pan down in front of Bacon for the dog to lick clean.

Smiler said gratefully, "I was very lucky to meet you, Professor."

The man smiled through his beard. "You were, Samuel. You were. But do not judge the rest of the human race by me – otherwise you'll be in for disappointments. Yes, you were very lucky. Right – now we'll strike camp and go and make your travel arrangements. *Caledonia stern and wild waits to greet the runaway child.*"

"I'm not a child," said Smiler stoutly.

The Professor grinned. "For the sake of the rhyme you have to be. No offence intended. Now you take the canopy down and I'll pack up the old pram."

So the two of them set about striking camp. When it was all done, with everything stowed away in the pram, the Professor with Smiler's help cleaned up the camp site, poured water over the fire embers and finally left the place neat and tidy.

It was very soon clear to Smiler that the Professor knew every inch of the countryside in this area. Pushing the pram along small tracks and paths, and occasionally lifting it over a stile or locked gate, they went away across a long stretch of heath and woodland. Finally, after a long climb to the head of a small valley, they came out on to a wide reach of flat grasslands which was traversed by a small, high-hedged dusty road.

On the road Smiler took over the pushing of the pram while the Professor walked at his side and gave him a running commentary on everything which they passed. He knew the name of each bird, each flower, bush and tree. And Smiler, walking with him, thought what a nice but odd sort of man he was. He was the kind, he thought, that old Joe Ringer back in Wiltshire would have liked. But Joe Ringer and all his time in Wiltshire now seemed a long way behind. Ahead of him lay Scotland, October and his father. Three pounds from his twenty would leave him seventeen pounds. That would be more than enough to keep him going until he found a job.

A mile down the road they came to a level-crossing. To one side of the red and white gates stood a tall signal-box and someway beyond it Smiler saw the platform and buildings of a small station.

The Professor said, "You wait here, Samuel, while I go and have a talk with an old friend. But first the money. A little grease to oil the wheels of commerce."

From his back pocket Smiler pulled out the stout brown envelope in which he kept his money. He slipped three notes out and handed them to the Professor. Then he put the envelope back in his pocket.

Smiler and Bacon sat on the grass at the side of the road while the Professor went along to the signal-box and climbed the steps to the control room at the top. He went in and Smiler could see him talking to a man in shirtsleeves.

After a little while the Professor came back, smiling and nodding his head.

"Is it going to be all right?" asked Smiler.

"It is, Samuel. *The great iron road to Scotland lies*

ahead – and you will travel it on a moving bed. Not bad. Not good. In between. That's the trouble with my poetry. Now then, we've got to wait until nine o'clock tonight. I'm going on into the village to stock up with provisions. Give me a pound and I'll bring some back for your journey."

"Would you, Professor?" Smiler fished for his brown envelope again.

"Of course. A small service gladly performed. Meanwhile you make yourself scarce around here. Keep off the road and be back just before sunset."

Smiler said, "Of course. But, Professor, while you're in the village could you get me an envelope and some paper and a stamp? I got an urgent letter to write."

The Professor's eyes twinkled. "Correspondence, eh? *Some brown-skinned, bright-eyed girlfriend – don't grieve for me, darling, we'll meet in the end?*"

Smiler chuckled and shook his head. "No – I got to write to my Sister Ethel that I'm supposed to live with while my Dad's away. I got to let her know I'm all right."

"Of course you have. Highly commendable behaviour," said the Professor and he set himself behind the pram and with a wave of his hand began to push it over the level-crossing.

Smiler watched him go. Then he turned back up the road with Bacon at his heels and went through the first gap in the hedge. Scotland, he thought. He was really going to Scotland. Things were turning out well, and the best turn-out had been meeting the Professor. That was a real stroke of luck.

At eight o'clock Smiler returned to the level-crossing. The Professor was sitting on the grass bank waiting for him. From the pram he produced a load of provisions for Smiler. As Smiler packed them into his haversack, the Professor said, "You've everything you need there for a two-day journey. Got you a couple of bottles of water, but go easy on it. You might or might not get a chance to fill up along the way. The packet of dog biscuits is because I presumed your four-footed friend is going with you."

"Well, yes, of course," said Smiler. Somehow it had never occurred to him that he would do anything else but take Bacon. They were both wanderers, had both been "destination unknown" types when they had met.

When he had finished his packing, Smiler wrote his letter to his Sister Ethel which the Professor promised to post for him.

The letter read: *Dear Sis, I am O.K. and doing fine but until Dad comes back I got to keep out of the way. Don't worry for me I have a dog now who is a faythfill freind, and others what are helping me along the road. Tell Albert hello and love to you both. Samuel. I am alright for money as well. S.*

When the light began to go from the sky and the last skylark had ceased its chorusing and dropped to the ground, the Professor said, "Time to move. *The shades of night are drawing nigh – Time for friends to say goodbye.*"

The Professor pushed his pram into the cover of some bushes. Then the two of them walked down the track past the signal-box and took up position on a steep embankment outside the little railway station. Here, alongside the main tracks, was a long length of track which made a shunting bay. The Professor explained that twice a week a northbound goods train came up the line and pulled into the bay around nine o'clock. It stayed for about fifteen minutes to let main line traffic through and then drew out to continue its journey northwards. The signalman in the box, having been paid, would turn a blind eye while Smiler selected a wagon and climbed aboard. All Smiler had to watch out for was that the crew of the diesel engine and the guard did not see him.

"Which they won't," said the Professor, "because they always use this break to have their supper."

Ten minutes later, the goods train pulled in, hauling behind it a long line of open and closed wagons.

The Professor, who was clearly very knowledgeable about trains, said, "Closed wagons no good. Locked. Open ones are the ticket this time of the year. Well ventilated but protected from the weather by their tarpaulins. But you don't want coal or machinery. Makes hard lying." He eyed the long line of wagons and then nodded. "Don't worry. I've spotted one for you."

He stood up and looked up to the engine and then down to the guard's van. There was no sign of the engine crew or guard. He began to move down to the line and Smiler and Bacon followed him.

Smiler's heart was thumping a little fast now. He'd hitchhiked plenty of times, and ridden buses dodging the conductor to avoid paying a fare – but he had never jumped a train before. He had read plenty of stories of people who had. Sometimes they could only manage to get underneath the truck and then they often fell and had a leg chopped off by the wheels.

They stopped close to an open wagon which had a green canvas tarpaulin over the top. The Professor squinted at the ticket on the side.

"This will do." He reached up, a knife suddenly in his hand, and cut one of the holding ropes of the tarpaulin. "I'll give you a leg up. You wriggle under and then I'll pass the dog up. All right?"

In the growing dusk, Smiler looked up at him and said, "Yes, Professor. And thank you very much for your help."

"Nothing at all, boy. Nothing at all. Adversity brings out the common humanity in us all. Now then, up you go!"

As Smiler reached for a hold on the truck, the Professor crouched down and gave him a bunt up with his shoulder. He then steadied him with his hands as Smiler crawled in. Smiler went under the canvas like an eel and tumbled into the wagon on to a layer of smooth sacks – which he found later contained agricultural fertilizers. He crouched on the sacks and shoved his head and shoulders back through the canvas opening and reached for Bacon as the Professor held the dog up.

Smiler hauled Bacon in and then popped his head out again to say goodbye to the Professor.

The Professor stood outside in the gloaming, his bowler hat cocked to one side, his big black beard teased by the light breeze of the evening, his bright eyes twinkling. Smiler liked him so much that he half thought of suggesting that the Professor should come with him. With someone like the Professor around there wouldn't be any trouble that could not be overcome. They could camp out on the mountains of Scotland and look after themselves easily. He was about to put this to the Professor when the man said, "Goodbye, Samuel. Keep a cool head and a steady hand. And give my qualified regards to Scotland. *By brae and burn and lonely glen – Who knows when we'll meet again?* Not good. Not bad either for this time of night. God keep you, my boy."

The Professor gave something suspiciously like a sentimental sniff, doffed his bowler regally, and then turned away.

Smiler said, "Bye, Professor. Thanks for . . . for everything."

Smiler watched the Professor move up the embankment and then become lost in the shadows of the trees at its top. Smiler ducked under the canvas and in the semi-darkness began to make himself comfortable, stacking aside some of the sacks to make himself a space to lie in, settling Bacon down with a big dog biscuit, and telling himself what a bit of luck it had been meeting the Professor.

Ten minutes later the goods train pulled out of the siding and hit the main track north. And five minutes later Smiler – always methodical – in checking over his possessions discovered that the brown envelope with his money in it had disappeared from his pocket.

For a moment or two he couldn't understand it. He was always careful with his money and he knew that he always buttoned his back pocket when he put the envelope in. He sat there, listening to the *rump-bump-rump* of the wheels over the rail joints and stared at the shadowy form of Bacon, crunching away at his hard biscuit.

Suddenly he said aloud to himself, "Of course!

That old Professor. He nicked it. Cool as a cucumber. He nicked it when he bunted me up. The old devil . . . !" For a moment or two he didn't know what to feel or think. Nearly twenty quids' worth up the spout. Then, suddenly, he rolled over on the sacks and began to laugh, telling himself, "Samuel M., you was done. He turned you over as neat as neat. But it don't matter, Samuel M. The only thing that matters is Scotland. You can get a job there and earn some more money."

Laughing still he rolled over and grappled with Bacon, the two of them mock fighting, as the train clattered steadily northwards.

3

∾ Operation Grey Goose ∾

The goods train was not a fast one. During that night it frequently drew off the main line to let passenger trains go through. Once during the night Smiler poked his head through the canopy while they were going slowly through a station and he caught the name – Penrith. It meant nothing to him except that he was pretty sure that it wasn't a Scottish one because it was too soon to be in Scotland yet.

He and Bacon slept on their smooth sacks. Now and again Smiler would wake to hear the *clackety-clack-clackety* of the wheels over the rails and to feel the wagon sway and swing below him. At first light he woke, feeling stiff and cold. He poked his head out to find a fresh dawn breeze cold on his face. There was a rose-pearl flush in the eastern sky against which was silhouetted a line of bare, grey-shadowed hills. Shivering, Smiler ducked below to escape the morning chill. He and Bacon had breakfast from the provisions which the Professor had bought. Smiler drank from one of the water bottles and he poured some of it into the inside of his cap for Bacon to drink. Luckily Bacon was very thirsty and lapped it up before much of it could soak away through the lining. Despite the breakfast, which Smiler thought would have warmed him up, he found that he was still shivering. It was so bad sometimes that his teeth rattled together and his body trembled all over as though someone were giving him a good shaking. Within the next hour things got worse. He had a bad pain in his stomach, his head began to ache, and now and then, instead of shivering, he went hot all over. In fact he felt very queer indeed. All he could do was to lie with Bacon huddled close to him and think how miserable he was.

Sometimes he found himself talking out loud to himself or to Bacon.

"Samuel M., you've ate something bad. I only hope it don't turn to a touch of the collywobbles. Not here."

He lay there, half-awake, half-asleep, his body going hot and cold, and his mind beginning to wander a little like it did just before going off to sleep so that things that started out sensibly slowly turned into nonsense. Fever, he thought. He'd had something like this once before when he was at his Sister Ethel's house. For a while he wished he were there now. Warmly tucked up in bed with Sister Ethel to look after him. "Say you was to die, Samuel M.? You might be here for weeks till they found you with the faithful hound beside you." Then the awful thought struck him that, maybe, as well as pinching his money, the Professor had poisoned his food. The Professor was a mad man, perhaps. Going about robbing and killing boys. . . .

Slowly Smiler passed into an uneasy feverish half-awake half-asleep dream. He lay in the wagon while the train went steadily north through Dumfries, Kilmarnock, Motherwell and into Glasgow. Here, without Smiler knowing a thing about it, except for the bangings and shoutings that came through into his dreams, the train was broken up. The wagons

34

were shunted and reshunted and a new train formed. At six o'clock that evening the train pulled out of Glasgow (where lower down the River Clyde lay Greenock to which his father was to return in October) and headed even farther northwards, rattling and swaying towards the highlands of Scotland.

Once, just before dark, Smiler came round, feeling a little better. He sat up and gave Bacon a drink and some dog biscuits. But he could neither eat nor drink himself. After this he lay back and dozed off. This time he dropped into a deep sleep, untroubled by dreams.

Smiler woke to hear Bacon whining gently. Then, in the darkness, the dog licked his face. He sat up and was pleased to find that, although he felt a bit as though he'd been pummelled all over, his head was clear and the hot and cold shivering fits had left him. And then he realized something else. The train was not moving and there was stillness all around.

Slowly, Smiler got to his feet and poked his head out of the wagon. It was a still clear night with a blaze of stars overhead. The truck stood in a siding with three others, but there was no sign of the rest of the train. Smiler decided that, whether he was in Scotland or not, he had had enough. He gathered up his belongings, lowered Bacon over the side, and dropped down after him.

Together they went across the waste ground at the side of the rails, climbed a fence and then dropped down a steep grass slope to find themselves on a road. Smiler looked up at the stars, found the North Star, and saw that the road ran west and east. He went westwards along it, Bacon at his heels, and after about half a mile came to a junction with a larger road. A signpost pointing south read – *Fort William 4 miles*. Smiler, having no idea what time it was, but knowing it must be very late because there was no traffic about, decided to make for Fort William.

He was feeling much better now and, as he walked, he took stock of his situation. He must have been in the truck a long time . . . a night and a day and almost another night. With luck he must be in Scotland. Sharp against the starlit sky he could see hills around him. He had a sack of provisions, the clothes he stood up in, Bacon for company and – how much money?

He turned out his pockets. There was a loose pound note in his trouser pocket and a handful of silver change among which were two fifty-pence pieces. Altogether he had nearly three pounds. Well, that wasn't too bad. He was already feeling better. It was clear to him now that after all that rain and sleeping out in that drainpipe he had caught a feverish chill. Yes, he was feeling much better and, what was more, hungry. But he wanted something better than sardines and bread. A proper breakfast, like the one the Professor (that old devil) had provided. Eggs and bacon and hot coffee! His mouth watered. There might be an all-night café in Fort William. If not, he would have to wait until morning. He moved down the road, his spirits returning, Bacon trotted at his heels and, from somewhere away to his right, came the cry of a nightbird which he recognized at once from his days with Joe Ringer. It was the whistle of a lone flying curlew.

* * *

Smiler, in fact, kept clear of Fort William until the sun came up. If he walked around the place on his own at night, he had decided, he might be spotted by some curious policeman. Breakfast would have to wait until the proper time.

When he did go into the town that morning it took him no time at all to realize, from the way the people spoke, that he was in Scotland. He knew the accent well because there was a Scottish family that lived next door to Sister Ethel. And all the things in the tourist shops told him that it was Scotland: the dolls dressed in tartan kilts and the picture postcards. The town itself stood on the side of a great loch with mountains on both sides. He found an early-opening lorry drivers' café and went in for breakfast. While he ate, he decided that he must buy a map. From his expeditions with his father he was fond of maps and could read them well. He had already seen one in the window of a newsagent's shop. The price marked on the cover was fifty pence. As he ate he debated with himself whether he would buy it or go in, say for a box of matches, and nick it. After a time he decided that, since he was in Scotland and in a way making a fresh start, he would buy it. It would make a hole in his funds, but he was sure that he would soon get a job somewhere. On a farm if he could. He didn't want any town job. No, thank you. He wanted a job where there wouldn't be too many people about to ask awkward questions.

By half past nine he was sitting on a seat on the town promenade that overlooked the loch, studying the map he had bought. He soon found Fort William and saw that it stood at the head of Loch Linnhe where the Caledonian Canal started running up through Loch Lochy and Loch Ness to Inverness. But the thing that surprised him was how far north Fort William was from Glasgow. It was miles away. Still, that was no worry. He had until October to get back to Glasgow and then Greenock.

By half past ten Smiler and Bacon had walked back through the town and northwards to where another road ran off westwards along the shores of another loch, called Loch Eil. Smiler had picked this road because eventually it reached the sea. If he couldn't get a farm job along the way, well, he might get something in a fishing village on the coast.

By eleven o'clock Smiler and Bacon had got a lift in a ramshackle farm lorry that took them well along the road and finally dropped them at a place called Glenfinnan. Smiler and Bacon walked onwards for another two hours but it was hard going because the road was narrow and full of holiday traffic. Smiler decided to turn off down a side road as soon as he could.

By six o'clock that evening Smiler and Bacon – on Smiler's own admission – were well and truly lost. They had taken a side road that led up through the lower slopes of the hills to the south. At first the rough road ran through growths of rowan and birch trees. After a time these were left behind and they were out on long stretches of grassland where small parties of sheep with grown lambs grazed. Smiler had decided to ask at the first farm he came to for work. But they passed no farm. They came to a fork in the road on a flat bluff covered with worn grey rocks. There was no signpost, so Smiler tossed up for it and took the righthand fork. It began to drop down through a narrow valley. High above it were steep heather-covered slopes with racing cloud shadows darkening their purple sweeps. The road grew rougher and narrower, dwindling now to a path more than a road, and a small burn ran alongside it. Smiler and Bacon followed this track for over an hour, sometimes going up and sometimes going down, sometimes parting with the burn but always meeting it farther on. As the track grew slimmer, the burn grew wider and became a small river. Quite a few things watched Smiler and Bacon pass by.

From a tall pine a pair of hooded crows saw them. Couched in bracken on the slopes high above, a roe deer doe with month-old twin calves saw them both, and a golden eagle, circling so high against the sun that Smiler could never have seen him, watched the movement of Bacon on the track and the human being with him.

An hour later when Smiler had told himself ruefully that he was getting nowhere fast, the track dropped steeply into a narrow, tree-lined glen where the small river rushed over a rocky bed in noisy turmoil. Smiler and Bacon came out of the trees at the foot of the glen to find themselves on a loch shore. There was not a house or a human being in sight, and Smiler groaned at the thought of having to go all the way back along the track. To his right the loch ran away into the distance and disappeared into a grey haze from which rose the dark slopes of a range of mountains. To his left the loch reached back into the hills for about a mile and then swung away at an angle sharply so that the rest of it was hidden from him by a steep craggy shoulder of hill. The loch itself was so wide that the far shore, he guessed, had to be more than a mile away.

Smiler sat down in a grassy hollow above the shore and consulted his map. Unfortunately it was a large-scale map. Although he could pick out where he had turned off the main road he couldn't find any track marked after the righthand fork he had taken. And as for the loch – the whole map where he thought he might be seemed to be a blue-marked patchwork of lochs. Stumped for the moment as to what to do, Smiler untied his haversack and he and Bacon had a meal. After the meal they stretched out in the sun and slept, both of them tired out from their long walk.

*　　*　　*

While Smiler and Bacon slept, a little farther down the lochside an old greylag gander was paddling quietly along the shoreline, dipping his long head and neck below the surface from time to time to root and feed in the thin carpet of underwater vegetation. The greylag was a prisoner of the loch for, though it could swim and paddle quite easily and walk when it went ashore, it could not fly. Its left wing had been broken close to the body. When it swam or walked the wing dragged loosely and awkwardly at the side of its body. The greylag had spent the winter on the loch and the moorlands above it. Early in the year it had taken off with its companions to make the long journey north to its Arctic breeding grounds. As the small skein of birds had moved down the loch a golden eagle, not yet a year old, had stooped at the geese.

The leader, seeing the eagle coming, had raised a quick *gang-gang-gang* alarm call and the skein had scattered in all directions. The young eagle diving downwards had been confused by the sudden wild scattering of the geese and had lost sight of the goose it had marked out for its prey. It had come out of its swoop and swung in a low curve at the nearest bird which it had hit clumsily on the left wing but failed to grasp with its talons. The injured goose had plummetted to the water and the golden eagle had soared upwards in vain pursuit of the wildly scattered skein of birds.

Unable to fly the injured greylag had been forced to stay on the loch. Over the months a great many animals, and a few people, had become aware of its presence. But none of them had ever been able to come near it. Disabled, it had learnt new cunnings and each night it roosted well out in the loch on a lonely pinnacle of a small rock island.

The greylag came now up the loch shore to the little sandy stretch of beach above which Smiler and Bacon slept in their grassy hollow. The bird knew the beach well. At the far end there was a growth of reeds and rushes where food could be found. On the shore above the reeds, too, was a wide stretch of rich grass on which it often grazed.

This day the gander paddled past the beach and foraged for a while in the rushes. Then, after taking a good look at the lochside, it went quietly ashore towards the grass, its left wing dragging awkwardly. As it did so the greylag was watched by an animal that had often seen it before, an animal that had once or twice stalked it but had never been able to get close to it.

In a wind-stunted oak close to the mouth of the river which ran into the loch, a wild cat was lying sunning itself in the crotch of a branch. The wild cat had been there a long time. It was a female with young kittens that waited for it now in their lair deep in the heart of a rocky cairn on the hillside above the river.

The wild cat had seen Smiler and Bacon pass by and disappear into the grassy hollow beyond the beach, and then had seen the greylag working its way up the shore line. Curled up in the angle of the tree trunk and the branch, its grey-brown streaky coat merged in a perfect camouflage against the weathered bark. With close-lidded amber eyes it watched the greylag finally come ashore and begin to graze on the grass ten yards from the water's edge. The wild cat watched for a time and then saw that the usually cautious greylag was slowly grazing farther and farther from the water.

The cat rose, arched its back and stretched its legs, and then dropped quietly to the ground on the far side of the tree. It was a big female, weighing over twelve pounds. Slowly it began a long stalk of the feeding greylag, keeping as close to the loch edge as it could so that it would eventually come between the water and the greylag. It moved – a grey-brown shadow, short ears close to its flat skull – foot by foot closer to the greylag, taking advantage of every heather and bracken patch and inching across the more open ground pressed tightly to the thyme-studded grass. Within five minutes it was only a couple of yards from the greylag, hidden behind a weathered piece of old tree-trunk drift stranded on the shore by the last high water rise of the loch. It eyed the greylag, marking the dragging left wing, the flesh-coloured bill and feet, the ashy, greyish-brown plumage and the dull white belly and white tail tip as the unsuspecting bird moved a little closer to the piece of old drift wood. Suddenly the wild cat's mouth opened, moving in a silent spasm of excitement, and its hind-quarters rose slightly and waggled as the strong rear legs drove against the ground and launched it into a fast running leap. The cat landed square on the back of the bird, its claws raking at the plumage, its mouth clamping on the base of the long neck. There was a scurry of grey and brown feathers as the greylag was bowled over. The gander hissed with fear and then gave a long, panicking *gang-gang-gang* call of alarm.

The noise woke Bacon immediately. He jumped up and barked and saw at once the confusion of fur and feather on the sweep of grass by the lochside. Catching at once the strong smell of cat, Bacon raced towards the fight, barking as he went.

His barks woke Smiler. He sat up sharply. For a moment his eyes were dazzled by the westering sun, and he wondered what on earth was happening. He was so dazed with sleep that for a moment or two he could not remember where he was. Then he saw Bacon racing towards the cat and the greylag.

Smiler jumped to his feet and went after Bacon. Long before he reached the patch of grass the fight was over. Clamped as it was to the bird's back, the wild cat had seen Bacon coming. It leaped away, turned for a second arching its back and lofting its tail as it spat defiance at Bacon, then it raced along the shoreline and reached its tree yards ahead of the dog. It went up the trunk and lodged itself in the highest branches while Bacon circled round and round below, barking and growling.

When Smiler reached the greylag it was lying on

43

its side, its broken wing spread awkwardly out from its body, paralysed with fright. The ground around it was covered with feathers and wisps of down from the bird's breast. Smiler bent down and picked the bird up. He guessed at once that something was badly wrong with its wing. He settled the wing gently against the bird's flank and cradled it in his arms. For a moment or two the greylag struggled and hissed and then was silent, fear and shock overcoming its natural instinct to struggle for freedom.

Far up the beach Bacon was still barking and dancing around the tree. Smiler, who had seen the wild cat streaking away, shouted to Bacon. Bacon came reluctantly back, turning every now and then to eye the tree and to growl menacingly. When Bacon reached Smiler, the greylag struggled wildly at the sight of the dog. But Smiler held it gently, talked to it and finally the bird settled down in his arms, giving an occasional loud hiss if Bacon came too close.

So, there was Smiler standing on the edge of the great loch, lost, with not a house or a human in sight, and with an injured bird in his arms, a bird that he was pretty sure if released would not survive long. Softly he caressed the bird's neck and back. He liked animals and the sight of one in distress always upset him.

He stood now with the bird in his arms and said, "Samuel M., here's a proper do. You don't know where you are and you got an invalid on your hands." Then to the greylag, he said, "And you stop hissing at Bacon. Weren't for him you'd be a goner."

It was at this moment that a noise came to his ears. It was a gentle *put-put-putting*. He looked up and saw coming down the loch, about two hundred yards away, a small boat with an outboard motor.

Smiler went down to the water's edge and, holding the greylag with one firm arm and hand, took off his cap and waved it, shouting at the top of his voice. The boat proceeded serenely up the loch. For a while Smiler thought that he was not going to be seen. There was only one person in the boat, sitting at the stern and steering. Then, when the boat was a good way out and almost past him as he shouted and waved, he saw it alter course.

The boat came slowly into the shore. As it entered the shallow water the person at the stern cut out the motor and tipped the engine forward so that the propeller should not foul the bottom. As the boat ran straight into the beach the helmsman jumped overboard into a foot of water and dragged the bows up on to the sand.

The person turned and faced Smiler. It was a girl. She was about the same height as Smiler and, he guessed, about his own age. She wore a floppy green beret with a yellow bobble on top and her long hair was tied at the back of her neck with a yellow ribbon. Her smooth skin was as brown as a berry and she wore a loose grey jersey and blue denims rolled up to her knees to show bare legs and feet. She was a pleasant looking girl with dark brown eyes. Bacon went up to her and sniffed at her bare legs and she put down a hand and teased one of his ears as though she had known him all her life.

She said, "What are you doing here?" She had a nice, soft, Scottish accent.

"I'm lost," said Smiler. "And this here is a injured bird. Some old cat thing went for it just

45

now. Bacon chased it off, but I think it got its wing broken."

The girl came up close and looked at the bird and then said, "No old wild cat did that. That's Laggy. We've tried to get him often but he never lets you get near. Had that broken wing for months, poor laddie." She gently touched the white nail on the tip of the gander's pink beak and went on, "Where you from?"

"England," said Smiler.

The girl laughed. "I can tell that from your voice. But England's a big place. What's your name and how did you get here?"

"I'm Samuel Miles. But how I got here is a long story."

"Then save it for some other time. We've got to do something for poor old Laggy. Come on, we'll take him to the Laird."

"Who is the Laird?" asked Smiler.

"Who is the Laird?" The girl echoed him, and then laughed. "You are a stranger around here for certain. The Laird is the Laird. He owns this beach we're standing on, the whole loch and half the mountains around."

"Gosh, he must be a very rich man."

"Rich, aye. But not in silver. Come on, in you get. By the way –" her face went suddenly serious as though she were aware that she had been lacking in courtesy – "I'm Laura Mackay. My father farms down the far end of the loch." She reached her hand out and took Smiler's. She gave it a shake that crushed his fingers.

Laura Mackay pushed the boat back a little way into the loch and Smiler, holding the greylag, waded through the shallow water and got in. Laura slipped

46

an arm round Bacon and lifted him aboard. Then she got aboard herself, went to the stern and lowered the outboard motor and started it. They circled away from the beach in a tight curve and began to move up the loch. In the bottom of the boat, Smiler noticed, there was a small battered suitcase and three large, bulky sacks.

From the shore the loch had looked quite smooth. As they moved out on to it Smiler found that there was quite a wind blowing and driving up a long series of choppy waves. Now and again one of these would smack against the bows and come spraying back over them. So far as Laura was concerned, Smiler noticed, she seemed unaware of the flying spray.

It was getting late now and the westering sun, although it held the southern shore of the loch in bright light still, had thrown dark shadows over the side on which Smiler had been resting with Bacon. The south shore was mountainous. Steep crags and cliffs came right down to the water's edge. As it was impossible to talk above the noise of the motor and the loud *smack-smack* of the waves against the bows, Smiler sat in silence, nursing the injured greylag, and watching the moving shores of the loch. It seemed a very long time since he had got off the train at Fort William that morning. The day had gone by like a kind of dream so that up until now it hadn't really come home to him that he was actually in Scotland. But he knew he was there now, with the fresh loch spray dewing his face, the stiff breeze flattening his anorak against his body and, everywhere he looked, rowan- and pine-marked crags and cliffs and beyond them the rising sweeps of mountains.

There was a touch on his shoulder from behind.

He turned to find the girl holding a sweet bag to him. He dipped in a hand, took one, and gave her a nod of his head in thanks. It was a peppermint and he sat sucking it happily. She was a nice girl, and he liked her. Crikeys, too, she was strong. She'd gripped his fingers as though she were going to break them off. A farmer's daughter, that was why. Probably helped her father about the place. Hard work. Work – that was what he had to find. He wondered if later he should ask her about a job with her father. But soon after he had finished the peppermint he forgot about work. Suddenly his stomach had turned a little queasy and he wondered if the movement of the boat was making him feel funny . . . seasick, maybe. Indignantly he told himself, "Don't be daft, Samuel M. How can you be seasick with your father a seaman, and this not the sea even?" But there was no doubt about it that he was feeling a little odd.

To take his mind off it, he kept his eyes fixed firmly ahead. They had now turned into that part of the loch which Smiler had not been able to see from the beach. As they moved up this arm of the loch, Laura kept the boat closer to the south shore to get more protection from the wind. Smiler could see a long way ahead a big island in the centre of the loch and a little way beyond it three smaller islands. From the big island the others all seemed to go down in size so that the last one was no more than a large stump of rock sticking out of the water.

Approaching the biggest island Smiler saw that it was faced with small cliffs on top of which grew stands of pine and other trees. Over these he could just glimpse the light of the sun touching grey slate roofs of what looked like towers of some kind. As they moved farther away from the south shore and out towards the island Smiler lost sight of the roofs. A handful of terns came hovering over them, some of them diving into the water to take small fish. Seeing them, Bacon stood up and barked. The noise made the greylag struggle a little in Smiler's arm, but he held the bird firmly and tried not to take any notice of the funny feeling in his head and stomach. Even if he were a little seasick he wasn't going to show it in front of a girl.

Behind him Laura, her face wet with water, her grey jersey spangled with it, put over the tiller and ran the boat closer to the craggy shore of the island. She motored the length of the island and then rounded its far end to give Smiler a view that he would never forget.

They swept round a small cliff and before them was a wide bay biting into the island, finishing in a semi-circular sweep of sand and pebble beach. From the beach the ground ran back in a flat meadowland of grass, then rose steeply through a scrub of juniper and yellow blooming bushes of whin to a small wood of silver birch and rowan trees behind which rose the bulwark of a tall wall made out of great stone slabs. Above the wall, like an illustration from some fairy tale, stood a castle. Smiler's eyes widened at the sight. It had round towers at each corner and a larger central one and they were all capped with conical, grey-slated roofs. Some of the windows were no more than slits in the walls, others were large and three-pointed, like church windows, and the higher ones had stone balconies. From one of the towers a flag was flying, a flag with a blue ground and a white saltire cross, the flag of St. Andrew. From one corner of the castle a long flight of steps zigzagged its way down and finished in a small stone jetty that reached out into the waters of the bay.

Behind Smiler, Laura cut the motor. As the boat headed silently to the jetty steps she said, "There's the flag flying. The Laird always flies it for me when I come up. And there's himself, too, waiting on the jetty. Now don't you move until I'm alongside and she's fastened properly. We don't want to lose poor old Laggy now we've got him."

Smiler hardly heard what she said. Turning into the bay the force of the wind and waves had been cut and they moved across calm water. He stared at the castle as though he were seeing something in a dream, some place of legend. And oddly, he felt that he *might* be dreaming for his head seemed as though it had floated a little way free of his shoulders and his body felt as though at any moment it would float up and try to rejoin his head. "Samuel M.," he told himself stoutly, "take a grip. You're still, maybe, a bit churned up with that chill you got in the drain pipe, or maybe it *is* seasickness. But whatever it is, you aren't going to show it in front of strangers. Particularly not if it *is* seasickness. What would your old man think?"

As he lectured himself, the boat drifted into the jetty. Laura held on to the rail of the bottom step, steadied the craft, and then jumped out with the stern painter and made it fast. Then she ran nimbly to the bows and grabbed the bow rope and made that fast. As she did so Smiler stared wide-eyed at the man who waited to greet them on the jetty steps.

Now, he told himself, he knew he was dreaming,

knew that it wasn't just light-headedness or seasickness, but that he must be in some crazy world of fairies and magic.

The man at the top of the steps was old and he was very tall and had long spindly arms and legs. He had a crop of loose white hair and a crop of even looser white beard. Above a kilt with a silver mounted sporran he wore a small, tight, green tweed jacket. On his legs were pinky grey woollen stockings with tartan tabs at the side. Down the right stocking a skean-dhu had been thrust, its handle just showing and glinting in the sunlight. Under his jacket he wore a tight black woollen sweater with a rolled collar close up under his beard. But the really astonishing thing about him was that he was covered with animals.

Smiler couldn't believe his eyes! On his right shoulder was a jackdaw. On his left shoulder sat a small brown owl. From one of his jacket pockets poked the head of a red squirrel and two white and brown piebald mice sat in the open gape of the other pocket. A small yellowy-brown bird, which looked to Smiler like a yellow-hammer but wasn't, sat on top of the silver mount of the sporran. And while Smiler watched, mouth open, there was a clap of lazy wings from the air above and a white fantail dove made a landing on the same shoulder with the jackdaw.

Laura glanced at Smiler and grinned at his surprise. Then she said, "We'll have to put a lead on your dog until he learns manners. Stay there till I explain things to the Laird."

She turned and ran up the steps to the man who gave her a shout of welcome, "Laura, my bonnie lass!" and clapped his arms around her so that all the birds on him went up in the air in a flurry of wings and the mice and squirrel disappeared into his pockets.

Laura said something to him which Smiler couldn't hear. Then she turned and came down and reached out for the greylag, saying, "Come and meet the Laird. You got a lead for the dog?"

Smiler nodded, fished in his pocket for Bacon's twine lead, and slipped it through his collar. He and Bacon stepped ashore and followed Laura up the steps.

The Laird watched him come, blue eyes twinkling under white eyebrows in the sun-and-weather-beaten face.

When Smiler reached the top step the Laird said – and for such a thin and spindly man his voice was surprisingly robust – "Well now, what has the girl brought this time? Always some lame duck – and very pleased I am to see old Laggy. We've wanted him for a long time. And – bless my sporran – a boy and a dog. A combination as old as time. And what do they call you, laddie?"

Overawed, and still feeling very seasick, Smiler said nervously, "Please, sir . . . my name's Samuel Miles and . . . and this is my dog. He's called Bacon. Bacon because –"

But Smiler never got round to explaining why Bacon was called Bacon. At that moment everything about him began to spin as though on a merry-go-round. The Laird, Laura, the birds and animals, and then the tall pines, the steps and the high towers of the castle, swooped round and round in a mad, giddy whirl until, with a little sigh of protest, Smiler closed his eyes against it all and collapsed gently at the Laird's feet and knew no more.

4

∽ *The Laird Defers a Decision* ∽

When Smiler woke the next morning it was to find himself in a strange bed in a strange room. It was a big fourposter bed with a red velvet canopy from the edges of which hung little gold tassels. The wooden posts at each corner of the bed had been carved with birds, beasts and flowers, with here and there the gnomish faces of merry little men and women peeping out from behind a flower or a bird. Smiler was lost in the bed. It was wide enough to hold four people with ease, and took up most of the space in the room, which was not a big one. In the wall across from the foot of the bed was a tall window, pointed at the top. The sun came streaming into the room to show up a badly worn carpet and two or three pieces of heavy oak furniture. Away to the right of the bed was a narrow wooden door, its hinges and fastenings made out of wrought iron.

Smiler lay there trying to sort out where he was and what had happened. Slowly the events of the previous day came back to him. He knew that he must have been still suffering from the chill he had caught and the sickness which had been with him during the railway truck ride. He was a bit fed up with himself for passing out at the feet of the Laird the moment he had met him. That was a pretty bad start, he thought. And in front of Laura Mackay, too. Samuel M., he told himself aloud, they'll think you're a real sissy.

He pulled himself up in the bed and it was then that he discovered that he was wearing pyjamas. They had red and white stripes and were miles too big for him. Somebody had folded the sleeve cuffs back to make them more comfortable, but underneath the bed clothes he could feel that his feet were trapped and tangled in the long length of the trousers. As he was struggling to get some freedom for his feet, the door opened and the Laird came in.

He was dressed exactly as he had been the previous day, but the wild population which inhabited his clothes and body had changed. There was a jay sitting on his right shoulder and a brown bantam hen on the other. The head of a black and white kitten peeped from one pocket. The flap of the other pocket was closed but Smiler could see the outside bulge and move as something stirred about within.

The Laird came up to the bed, gave him a beaming smile and said, "Well now, how's the invalid this morning?"

Smiler said, "I'm all right, thank you, sir. But I'm not really an invalid."

"Of course not, laddie. Just a touch of the over-doing-its. We gave you a glass of hot milk with a drop of malt in it and you curled up in bed like a dormouse in a nest."

"Malt, sir?" If there was one thing Smiler hated it was the cod-liver oil and malt which his Sister Ethel – who was old fashioned in her remedies – sometimes forced on him.

"Ay, malt, laddie. Whisky – the first medicine any true Scot turns to."

Smiler's eyes widened. "You mean I had whisky, sir?"

"Aye. Just a dram to drive out the shakes."

"Gosh. . . !" said Smiler. "That's what my father drinks sometimes."

"Then he's a wise man. Now what do you feel like doing? A few more hours there or get up?"

"I'd like to get up. . . . Oh, what about Bacon? I mean, sir, I hope he's been behavin' himself."

"No trouble. All animals have natural good manners. Leave 'em alone for a bit and they soon work things out for themselves. He's settling down nicely. Right then, you stay there until Laura's brought your breakfast and then you can get up. After that we'll go into a thing or two. The present is a fine and glorious thing but one must always keep a weather-eye on the future." For a moment he gave Smiler a quizzical look, his face growing serious, and then he suddenly winked and turned towards the door.

Smiler, who never had any trouble deciding very quickly whether he liked people or not, knew that he liked this tall, gaunt man. He said, "Please, sir, what's in that other pocket? Not the kitten one."

The Laird turned at the door. "Ye've a quick eye. That's Meggie." He put his hand into the pocket and pulled out a long length of grass snake, the animal's sleek body twisting and coiling around his hand and wrist, the blunt head weaving so that Smiler could see its white markings.

"Blimey!" said Smiler, delighted. "She's super, isn't she?"

"Aye, laddie, she's beautiful. I can see you know more than a little about animals."

"I like them, sir. You can always get on with 'em – if you takes your time and don't rush 'em."

"No truer thing was ever said." The Laird put

55

the grass snake back in his pocket, gave Smiler another wink and then was gone.

Smiler lay there, feeling his old self again, and thinking what a nice man the Laird was. Any man had to be nice that animals trusted like that. When he'd been in Wiltshire, before going on the run again, he had learnt that, and he'd learnt about animals too.* They were all nice, really. It was just that you had to learn to handle them properly.

A little later Laura came in with his breakfast tray. Smiler did full justice to the meal. He had coffee, and porridge with cream and brown sugar on it. Then came three boiled eggs with freshly baked bread and salty, tangy butter. After that he had the same bread spread with strawberry jam – but it was a different kind of strawberry jam from any Smiler had had before. Laura, sitting on the end of the bed and watching him eat, explained that it was made from the wild strawberries that grew in the meadow and banksides below the castle.

She was dressed as Smiler had seen her yesterday and she chatted to him as though she had known him for years. She was, Smiler soon realized, a real old chatterbox. All you had to do was to ask a question and she was away. Smiler soon knew a lot about her and about the Laird and the castle.

He learned that the Laird's real name was Sir Alec Elphinstone. He owned the loch and this castle, and acres and acres of the wild mountainsides around the loch. But none of the land brought him much money. A great deal of the land was let out to tenant farmers and the rents were very low. He also let the salmon and sea-trout fishing at the lower end

* See the first 'Smiler' book, *The Runaways*.

of the loch, but the part from where she had picked up Smiler, and right up to the far end beyond the castle, was never let because the whole of that area was kept as a wild life sanctuary. The Laird had been a surgeon in Edinburgh but had retired ten years ago when his wife had died. He had one son who was a Captain in the Royal Navy. On the island he kept all sorts of animals which had been injured and which he treated until they were well enough to go off and look after themselves.

"But the trouble is," said Laura, "lots of them don't go off. They get to like it here and just stay on. I come up once every week or so to bring him his post and supplies and usually stay a night and tidy things up. And it needs it. He's the most scattersome man I ever saw. I bring the animals up to him. The people around bring them into the farm. He doesn't like people up here. Not that he doesn't like folks. He's aye one for a ceilidh now and then –"

"A what?"

"A ceilidh. That's a party. Singing and dancing and – for some of them – a drop too much of the whisky. Like some of my brothers I could name."

And name them she did. She was the last child of five – all the rest boys. One of them worked on the farm with her father, one was a deckhand on a fishing trawler, and the other two were married, one a schoolteacher in Inverness and the other a sergeant in the Glasgow police force. (Smiler hoped that this brother would never come to hear about him!) She, herself, helped her mother in the house and also did some farm work. It was she who had baked the fresh bread that Smiler was eating. She always made a batch of loaves for the Laird when she came up.

Exhausting for the moment the subjects of the Laird, the castle and her family, she drew a quick breath, pushed the long brown hair back out of her eyes, and said, "And now what about you, Samuel Miles from England? What are you doing in Scotland? If it's no a rude question?"

For a moment Smiler was stumped. Then he said casually, "Oh, I'm kind of travelling. Seeing things until . . . well, until it's time to meet my father."

"What, all on your own? Just with a dog?"

"Why not? I can look after myself. I'm going to get a job, too. Maybe on a farm."

Laura laughed. "A lot of good you'd be if you go fainting all over the place."

"I didn't faint. I just . . . well, I'd just overdone it a bit. The Laird said so."

"Aye. He'd say anything that suited him. I'll warn you – he's got his eye on you. But maybe if it's a job you're after you won't mind."

"What do you mean?"

"You bide your time and see. But he lost Willy McAufee last week. Took off for a job in some factory in Fort William." She stood up. "Well, I can't sit here and listen to you chat all day. I've a few things more to do then I'm off back to the farm. The bathroom's just down the stairs outside and you'll find all your clothes there." She took the tray and gave him a cool, half-smiling look. "And just when and where are you meeting this father of yours?"

Smiler, after a moment's hesitation, said, "He's a cook on a cargo ship. I'm going to meet him at Greenock . . . fairly soon."

"And you've no mother or other family?"

Smiler, who was getting her measure, said with a grin, "I thought you had more things to do than listen to me chat."

Laura grinned too. "In other words, mind me own business. And why not, too? If there's one kind of body I can't bide it's the chattery, nosy-parker sort." She went to the door with the tray and called over her shoulder as she went out, "Bye. I'll be up next week sometime so I may see you – if you haven't taken off for Greenock."

Smiler found the bathroom and his clothes. The bath itself was ancient and rust-marked and big enough for a porpoise to swim in comfortably. Over the bath was a shower head and Smiler took a cold shower. The water was so cold that it made him gasp, but afterwards the whole of his body glowed and he felt a different person.

Back in his room, dressing, he smiled to himself at the thought of Laura's curiosity. She was as bad as his Sister Ethel. Looking out of the window he realized that his room was in one of the round towers. It had a view down over the castle wall to the beach and the small jetty. As he stood there, he saw Laura with the Laird at her side go down to the small boat. Bacon he saw was trotting happily at the Laird's heels.

For a moment or two the Laird and Laura chatted as she stood in the boat preparing to start the outboard motor. Smiler would have been interested if he could have heard the Laird speaking.

He said to the girl, "Thank you, Laura, my lass. Give my regards to your mother and father – and I'll see you next week sometime."

"I'll be up, Laird."

"Oh, and Laura –" the Laird put his foot on the bow of the boat ready to ease it off – "there's just one wee favour you can do me. Until you come up again it would be a kindness to me and mostly perhaps to him, if you said nothing about the boy being up here. Would you do that?"

Laura smiled and nodded. "Of course, Laird. You think he's in trouble?"

The Laird chuckled. "There's not a boy alive in the world who isn't in trouble of some kind. It's the nature of the animal." He pushed the bows out and stood and watched as Laura started the motor. The boat swung in a half circle and headed out of the bay and Laura gave a wave of a hand as she went.

From his window Smiler watched her go. To his delight he saw two fantails swoop down from the castle roof and circle round the boat until it reached the craggy point at the end of the bay. Then they came flying back and settled on the ground at the Laird's feet where Bacon took no notice of them at all.

* * *

It was some time before Smiler could find his way down from the tower to the main hallway of Elphinstone castle. The top part of the building was a maze of narrow, twisting stairways and stone-slabbed passages with here and there a lance-pointed window to light the way. Finally he came out on to a top landing, floored with great oak planks and lit by a big four-paned mullion window. On the walls were time-darkened oil paintings of men and women. Most of the women wore great sweeping dresses, their powdered hair piled high, and some of them

60

had children leaning against their knees and grey-hounds lying at their feet. The men – who mostly looked like the Laird – were young and old and a few of them wore tam o'shanters and kilts and carried bucklers and claymores. The bright sunlight through the window showed a fine layer of dust on the oak planks and the balustrades of the great wooden stairway that ran down to the main hall. The hall had a large refectory table running down the middle around which fifty people could have sat, and there were more oil paintings on the walls. Near the main door, which led out on to the terrace, was an ancient suit of armour, its chain mail and breast plates finely stippled with patches of rust. The whole place, Smiler told himself, would have made Sister Ethel's fingers itch to begin spring cleaning.

A big open stone fireplace took up part of one wall of the great hall. A couple of peat slabs smouldered in it on top of a pile of grey-white ash which had accumulated over the months. Sitting by the fire in a shabby wing-backed green velvet chair was the Laird. He was reading a newspaper. At the side of his chair on the dusty floor was a pile of other newspapers and letters which Laura had brought up to him. Lying in front of the fire as though he owned the place was Bacon. He looked up and thumped his tail in greeting as he saw Smiler. As Smiler went across to the Laird a white fantail flew through the open terrace door and perched on top of the suit of armour.

The Laird looked up, peering over the top of a pair of wire-rimmed spectacles he wore for reading.

"There you are, laddie. You managed to find your way down."

"Yes, thank you, sir."

"Well done. Many's the time in the past that we've had to send out search parties for guests lost somewhere between here and their bedrooms." He grinned. "A few we never found. They're maybe still wandering around somewhere in the corridors."

As Smiler chuckled, the Laird nodded to a chair on the other side of the fireplace and went on, "Sit ye down. I want to have a chat with you. A straight man-to-man talk."

Smiler sat on the chair and said, a little nervously, "Yes, sir. What about, sir?"

"About you, of course, Samuel Miles." He laid the newspaper on his lap. The bantam hen on his shoulder was sleeping cuddled against the side of the white beard. The jay on the other shoulder flew off with a flash of white and blue and disappeared through the terrace door. "This," said the Laird tapping the newspaper, "is *The Times* of London, two days old, brought up by Mistress Laura with my mail and the other back numbers of newspapers. Up here we have neither radio nor television. News comes slow but sure and I always read *The Times* diligently. Now, over my breakfast this morning, I came across a very interesting little piece in here –" he tapped the paper again "– very interesting. You'd do me a favour by reading it and then I'd appreciate your comments about its subject." He handed the newspaper over to Smiler who saw that a half-column had been ringed around with red pencil. "Take your time," said the Laird and he fished at his side for an unopened letter.

Smiler sat and read the report in the paper. As he had begun to suspect while the Laird had talked, it was about him and his exploits in Wiltshire. It told how he had been sent to approved school for stealing an old lady's handbag with twenty pounds in it at Bristol; how he had run away from the school and changed his name, dyeing his fair hair brown and hiding his freckles with dark sun-tan lotion, and had got a job as a kennel boy with two elderly Irish gentlewomen on the edge of Salisbury Plain. The article told how Smiler had lodged with a scrap-dealer and poacher called Joe Ringer and how the last thing that had been heard of Samuel Miles was that a truck driver had given him a lift northwards, and how he had disappeared one evening into the woods taking with him a stray dog, called Bacon, a small white mongrel, with a brown left ear, which walked with a limp.

Smiler finished reading the report and lowered the paper to his knees to find the Laird's bright blue eyes steadily on him.

The Laird said, "You're that Samuel Miles, laddie?"

"Yes, sir."

"Would you care to answer a few questions? Maybe one or two could be a mite personal."

"You can ask me anything you like, sir."

"Frankly answered. That's what I like. Right." The Laird reached out a foot and rubbed the recumbent Bacon on the shoulder. "How did our friend Bacon, here, come to change so quickly from a brown-eared limping white mongrel?"

"That must have been Mr. Bob, sir."

"Mr. Bob?"

"The truck driver. He was a nice man. He must have told the police wrong . . . on purpose perhaps, sir."

"On purpose of course, then. And how did you get to Scotland?"

"The Professor – he's another man I met – put me on a railway truck full of fertilizer sacks. I got off at Fort William. He was a nice man, too."

The Laird reached into his pocket and pulled out a pipe, a tobacco pouch and two piebald mice. He began to fill the pipe, eyeing Smiler, and the mice clambered back into his pocket. He said, "You've the knack of falling on your feet, it seems, and the knack of looking after yourself. Have ye the knack too of dipping your hand into other people's purses?" His voice was severe as he said this.

Smiler said quickly, "Of course not, sir. I used to nick a few small things from shops once. But not any more. And I never took the old lady's handbag. Never!"

The Laird lit his pipe and puffed a great cloud of smoke into the air. Then he said, "Show me the boy who hasn't nicked a few small things in his time and I'll look for the beginning of angel's wings on his back. Now tell me about the old lady."

"Well, sir, it was like this . . ."

Smiler told the story while the Laird puffed at his pipe, listening and nodding now and then. One afternoon in Bristol an old lady had been jostled off the pavement by a boy and her handbag stolen. A policeman seeing the act had gone after the thief. Rounding a corner he had seen a boy running down the pavement. The policeman had caught him and had found that he was holding the handbag with the money in it. The boy was one Samuel Miles. His father was away at sea and he was living with a married sister. Samuel Miles had been in some small bits of bother with the police before. But Samuel Miles' story now was that he had been standing just round the corner when a boy he knew had come rushing past him and had tossed him the handbag, shouting "Hide it!" The boy was one Johnny Pickering, and no friend of Samuel Miles. In fact they disliked one another. Samuel Miles said that he was caught running away because he was running after Pickering to make him take the handbag back. Both boys were the same height and both had fair hair. Samuel Miles had said that Pickering must have seen the following policeman and, once round the corner, tossed the handbag to him and escaped. But in the juvenile court the parents of Johnny Pickering had sworn that their son had been at home all the afternoon and that Samuel Miles was lying to save himself.

Smiler finished, "But I wasn't fibbing, sir. Pickering did it. They sent me to approved school and I escaped. I been running ever since in a way – because I know nobody can sort out the Pickerings but my Dad. When he comes back, he'll soon put it all right. And, until he does, I'm keeping away from that approved school. His boat – the *Kentucky Master* – docks in Greenock the beginning of October. I got to keep out of the way until then." Smiler stood up. "You don't have to tell the police, do you, sir?"

The Laird took the pipe from his mouth and pointed to Smiler's chair. "Put your bottom down on that again, laddie, and listen to me."

"Yes, sir." Smiler sat down.

"Now then, let's get a few things straight. First, I believe you didn't steal the bag. Second, are you sure your father can sort this thing out?"

"Oh, yes, sir. He'll know how to deal with that Pickering lot."

"Aye, I can imagine that. But October's a fair stretch away yet. What will you do until then."

"I'm going to find a job. I'm not afraid of work."

"So I gather. And you've a touch with animals, too, it seems. You must tell me about this cheetah business sometime, but that can wait for some evening over supper. Mistress Laura tells me your father's a ship's cook. What kind of cook are you?"

"Well, I'm not too bad, sir. Joe Ringer taught me a lot. Sir. . . ?" Smiler stood up, and then went on, "Was you thinking, maybe, of offering me a job here?"

The Laird shook his head. "No, lad, I wasn't thinking about it." Then, seeing the glum look on Smiler's face, he said, "I stopped thinking about it five minutes ago. You've got a job here –"

"Gosh! Holy Crikeys, sir – that's smashing!"

The Laird waved his pipe. "Sit down and stop dancing like a monkey. You've got a job here, where I can keep an eye on ye. You've got Willy McAufee's job, the daft unreliable loon who went off to Fort William a week ago. You'll get your board and lodgings. Cook as needed. Odd jobs as needed. Help look after the animals. Housework as needed – and by Saint Andrew, himself, it is needed. And anything else that is needed. By the time you've finished your day you won't want to do anything but fall into bed and sleep. And in return you get two pounds a week. And meanwhile I'll seriously consider the question of whether I should report your whereabouts to the police." His blue eyes twinkled suddenly. "At a conservative estimate I should think it will take me all of now until October to come to a decision. We Elphinstones were always long-winded ones for making up our minds. Now let's take a walk around the place and I'll show you your duties."

The Laird stood up and went to the terrace door. For a moment Smiler stared after him, hardly able to believe his luck. The Laird wasn't going to tell the police and he'd got a job! Just the kind of job he knew he would like. He jumped up from his chair and hurried after the Laird. Bacon rolled over to his feet and followed Smiler out into the sunshine of the grey-stoned terrace with the bright water-glitter of the loch stretching into the distance like a moving mirror.

*   *   *

For the next two hours the Laird took Smiler on a conducted tour of the island. At the far end of the beach a large area had been penned in with wire netting from the bed of the loch up to a height of four feet above water. It was here that the wild fowl lived. There were two great black-headed gulls that were recovering from the effects of oil pollution, a family of four young merganser ducks that had been abandoned by their parents which had either been shot or fallen prey to some marauding fox or wild cat, a pochard duck that had lost the sight of one eye from an attack by a hooded crow, and a dozen or so other water fowl, some of which were perfectly healthy. The Laird explained that there was no netting over the top of the extensive pen so that the birds were free to fly away when they were recovered or felt like it. The trouble was that a lot of the birds preferred to stay where they were. Some flew away during the day to feed up and down the loch and its shores and came back to roost at night. Some even raised their families within the pen. On little islands in the enclosure and along the reedy banks there were small rush-thatched houses for sleeping and breeding quarters. At the back of these were a few completely wired-in runs where new arrivals were kept. In one of these was the greylag gander which Smiler had brought.

"Later today," said the Laird, "we'll take him into surgery and see what we can do. The poor lad is as thin as a rake."

In one of the other special pens was a miserable looking heron which had broken its right leg and this was now splinted up.

"When I first started," said the Laird, "I used to treat broken legs with plaster. But the fool beasts thought it was something good to eat and would peck it all away till the point came when they would take a tumble on their heads and looked surprised. Now I know better. Always use a light wood splint."

On the far side of the castle, built up against the tall stone retaining wall, was a large aviary, and a set of wired runs for animals. In one of the runs was a young otter which had lost the foot from its left hind leg. In another was a large mountain hare with a wide bandage round its neck where it had been mauled before escaping from a fox. All these pens and runs Smiler was told it would be his duty to keep clean and the occupants fed and watered. But the more Smiler went round with the Laird the more he realized that there were far, far more healthy animals about than injured ones. A young roe deer moved freely among the scrub of the sharp pine-crowded rise at the back of the castle. Red squirrels scampered without fear among the branches and pigeons and doves hovered over their heads as they walked. Some settled now and then on the Laird, waiting for him to put his hand into his pocket and bring out corn for them to eat. Halfway up the slope in a small clearing there was a pile of beaten sand at the entrance to a badger's sett.

"That's where Bill and Jennie live," said the Laird. "I've had them five years and each autumn we ferry the year's young across to the lochside and turn them free. Otherwise we'd have a population explosion. You know, sometimes the little devils swim back. Did you know a badger can swim?"

"No, sir," said Smiler.

"Well then, learn this, laddie – whatever anyone else may say to the contrary there isn't a four-legged creature in the world that can't swim when it wants to. Now come with me and I'll show you one of the best swimmers in the world."

They climbed through the rising wood until they were above the level of the topmost turrets of the castle and then plunged down a steep slope until they were standing on a sheer crag top that faced southwards across the loch. Fifty feet below them was the clear water. The water was about twenty feet deep and Smiler could see every rock on the bottom.

The Laird lay down and pushed his head out over the fall and made Smiler do the same. He pointed out a large submerged rock a little way out from the foot of the crag.

"See behind it, laddie – that long grey shape. Looks like a sunk branch. But watch and you'll just spot the little movement, the waggle of its noble tail. That's a salmon. A big chap, about twenty pounds. Came in from the sea months ago, and he's waiting there for the autumn floods. When he feels the loch rise he'll be away and up the burn he was born in to find a mate and spawn. And good luck to him if he ever makes the sea again, for to be born and to beget and then to die is the usual lot of the salmon. Though a few make the spawning journey more than once. Usually the hen fish. One night I'll tell you all about the bonnie fish. See, away to his left there, two smaller shadows? They're sea-trout. I'll show you how to catch them."

Smiler, who was fascinated by fish and fishing, and had learnt something about both from old Joe Ringer, could have rested there longer watching the fish. But the Laird, whose ample years had not impaired his activity nor dimmed his love of talk, stood up and turned back to the castle.

As they entered the pine trees, a large, slow-moving golden labrador came slowly up the path to meet them.

"That's Midas," explained the Laird. "His eyes and his nose are as sound as they ever were but he's a wee bit deaf. So, if you walk up behind him unawares he takes it as kindness if you give a loud cough to warn him. If you don't, he's apt to turn and give your leg a nip – unless his nose has warned him in time that you're a friend. He and Bacon have already met."

They went back to the castle, and at the door to the great hall the Laird said, "As for the house, you can explore it for yourself and if you get lost I'll send Midas to sniff ye out. In the closet off the kitchen – that's way down in the bowels of the place – you'll find all the hard-weather clothes, gum boots and stout shoon you need. There's an accumulation of generations of Elphinstone gear there. Enough to fit an army. But, for the moment, let's concentrate on lunch. Bread and cheese and a bottle of beer for me. For yourself there's all the milk you can drink. Which reminds me, I didna show ye the cow. That's another job for you – the milking of her. I'll give you a lesson later today. Now, off with ye, and see what you can find in the kitchen. You've the eyes, ears and nose God gave you – they should lead you to all we want. Away with you now."

Slightly overwhelmed Smiler hesitated for a moment, then he said, "Yes, sir. I'll do my best."

"That's the spirit, laddie," said the Laird and he headed for his armchair and the remaining unopened letters and newspapers.

Smiler, with no idea where the kitchen was, went across the great hall and through the first door he saw. Overwhelmed, and a bit confused, he might be, but he remembered how in his last job in Wiltshire everything had seemed strange and a bit too much at first, yet within a few days he had everything sorted out and was feeling at home.

As he picked his way down a gloomy flight of stone stairs, hoping it would lead to the bowels of the castle and the kitchen, he said out loud, "Samuel M., just take it easy and use your loaf and things will sort themselves out." Then he chuckled, and putting on an accent added, "Ye canna do more than your best, laddie." Then the chuckle died and he groaned, "Oh, Holy Crikeys – milking a cow! How am I goin' to manage that?"

5

∽ *The Watcher from the Shore* ∽

It took Smiler some time to find the kitchen. Below
the main floor of the castle there was a warren of
storerooms, larders, dairy room, gun- and rod-room,
old-clothes- and boot-room, and a dozen other
rooms which at the moment he had no time to
explore beyond opening their doors and convincing
himself that they were not the kitchen. The kitchen
itself, when he found it, was a pleasant surprise. It
was long and low-ceilinged with a wide, curved
window cut through the solid rampart wall of the
castle to give a view out over the bay. There was a
long pinewood table (freshly scrubbed, like the rest
of the kitchen, by Laura) and chairs, dressers and
cupboards and rows and rows of crockery shelves.
All the cooking was done on a large butane gas
cooker – for which Laura brought up fresh fuel
containers once a month. In addition there was a
vast, wood-burning kitchen range and oven which
were seldom used. The water came from a pump
with a long handle that stood over a low stone sink.
Smiler could only guess that the water came from a
well down in the bowels of the castle's foundations
or else from the lake. On the cushions of the windowseat was a black and white cat with a litter of kittens
in an old wicker basket.

Smiler ferreted around the place and eventually
found all the supplies for a light lunch. He fixed up
the Laird's bread and cheese and beer on a tray and

carried it up to him and set it on the corner of the long refectory table near his armchair.

The Laird said, "Where are you going to have your bite, lad?"

Smiler said, "In the kitchen, if you please, sir. It's nice looking out of the window down there."

The Laird nodded. "Aye, it is. There is no better place to eat in a house than the kitchen, close to the heart of things. Breakfast and lunch you can take where and when the fancy strikes you, but at night we eat together – in the kitchen when we're alone, and up here if we are lucky enough to have company which is not often."

So Smiler went back to the kitchen and had his lunch on the windowseat with the cat and her kittens. When he had finished he collected the Laird's tray and then washed up the crockery in the big stone sink. After that he was a bit at a loss to know what he had to do so he spent some more time making himself familiar with the lower rooms of the house.

While he was doing this he suddenly heard the sound of a bell echoing and reverberating from the floor above.

He ran up to the main hallway to find the Laird standing at the foot of the grand stairway tugging away at the tufted end of a long rope which ran up through a hole in the ceiling to some invisible bell high in the top regions of the house.

When the Laird saw Smiler, he stopped ringing and said, "When the bell rings, work begins. But if it rings at night, you know the place is on fire or we're being attacked." He winked and went on, "Right, first to deal with old Laggy and then we'll introduce you to Mrs. Brown."

Surprised, Smiler said, "Mrs. Brown, sir?"

"The cow, lad. On account of her colour."

The Laird then led the way down into the bowels of the castle and through a maze of passages which Smiler had so far not discovered until they came finally to a small door that led out through the very bottom part of the rampart wall to the space set aside for the animal and bird pens. Beyond the pens and built against the wall was a long, low wooden hut with one big glass window in its front and three glass skylights on the roof. On the door was painted –

SURGERY: 24 HOUR SERVICE.

"That," said the Laird, "was painted on by my humorous minded son – himself a surgeon in the Navy. A man like your father, I imagine – only content when he's got good teak planking between himself and the sea. Now then, you get old Laggy and bring him along."

Smiler went off to Laggy's pen and brought him to the surgery. For the next half hour Smiler saw a different Sir Alec Elphinstone. The gander was placed on the bench in the spotless surgery and the Laird gave it an injection of some stuff with a name which Smiler could not remember. When the bird passed out, the Laird began to examine its broken wing. Smiler watched the gentleness and sureness of the man's hands with fascination. From the moment he began to deal with the bird it was as though the Laird had completely forgotten everything else in the world but the job before him. Although he talked to Smiler, explaining what he was doing and now and again asking him to pass things, his eyes never left the prostrate greylag. He located the break in the main wing bone, set it, and then splinted it up with light strips of thin wood which he taped into place. As Smiler helped him by holding and turning the goose, he bound the whole of the left wing against the bird's body with tape and bandages so that it could not move.

When the operation was over, the Laird said, "Right, Samuel M. – take him back and put him in the pen hutch. When he comes round he's on soft mash for a few days. In a month the wing will be as good as new. When you've done that we'll visit Mrs. Brown."

Smiler went off carrying Laggy whose head and neck hung limply over his arm. It was a few minutes before he realized that the Laird had called him Samuel M. The strangeness of it almost made him stop in his tracks. That was what his father alone called him! And the Laird couldn't possibly have known that. What a funny thing. Then, suddenly, he felt very pleased and very proud about it.

A short while after this, the thought of being called Samuel M. by the Laird was gone completely from his head because he found himself alone in the small pasture dealing with Mrs. Brown.

Mrs. Brown was a small cow with her right horn a little twisted. She had large, gentle eyes, a shiny brown coat and a long swishing tail. The Laird led him across the pasture to the cow and took her by the small rope halter she wore round her head. He led her to a small birch tree and fastened her to a short length of rope that hung from the tree.

"When she knows you – she'll stand for milking without the roping," the Laird explained. He sat down on a three-legged stool which they had brought

75

from the surgery together with a large milk bucket, and gave Smiler his first and only lesson in milking. With the pail under Mrs. Brown's udder, he showed Smiler how to hold a teat in each hand and work with a gentle but firm pulling and squeezing action so that the warm, sweet-smelling milk squirted into the pail. "Easy as falling off a log," he explained. "Just work your way around the bell-pulls and strip her out evenly . . . until there's no more to come. You'll have no trouble with her."

He sat Smiler down on the stool and stood by to monitor Smiler's first attempts and to advise him. Then, after a few minutes, he said, "Aye, you're doing fine, Samuel M. In a few days you'll have the touch of a master." And with that he walked off and left Smiler with Mrs. Brown.

While the Laird had been with him Smiler had felt reasonably unworried. But the moment he was on his own a hot sweat broke out all over him, and his hands became awkward and somehow unwilling to do the motions which the Laird had shown him. In addition, Mrs. Brown's manner seemed to change with being left alone to a stranger's manipulations. With the Laird she had been the most biddable cow in the world, standing quietly and chewing the cud contentedly. But a few moments after the Laird had gone her manner changed, and she started to play tricks. As Smiler leaned his head against her flank as the Laird had done, concentrating on the milking process, she suddenly switched her long tail round and hit him a crack on the face with the tufted tip. The blow was so unexpected that Smiler gave a sharp cry and fell backwards off the stool. As he lay in the grass Mrs. Brown looked round and stared at him in innocent surprise, as though she was wondering what he was doing.

Smiler got back on the stool and turned his head this time so that if she did flick him again it would not be on his face. Mrs. Brown did flick, three times, and Smiler took the blows stoically and said aloud, "You don't catch me like that again, old girl."

As though Mrs. Brown understood and wanted to show him what a novice he was, she gave a low moo and, with a short, swift kick of her nearside rear leg, knocked the milk bucket and stool over.

Smiler lay on his back with milk running around him and could have cried with despair. All that milk gone! But he pulled himself up and got back on the stool and said firmly to himself, "Serves you right, Samuel M. You had the bucket on the ground and not held between your legs like the Laird showed you."

This time he held the bucket firmly between his legs and began milking again. As though she understood that the kicking trick was out of the question, Mrs. Brown tried a tail flick or two. Smiler took the knocks with fortitude. Then Mrs. Brown suddenly twisted her head and long neck round, so that her muzzle was close to his face, and snorted a fierce warm burst of sweet cud-breath at him.

"Please, Mrs. Brown!" cried Smiler.

Mrs. Brown gave him another breath snort and then abruptly moved her rear quarters sideways two yards. Smiler was left sitting well away from her with the bucket between his legs and the teats gone from his hands. Sighing he dragged the stool and pail over to Mrs. Brown and went back to milking, but by now he was so flummoxed and hot that he could not remember which teats he had been working. In the next fifteen minutes Mrs. Brown kept him on the alert with tail switches, breath snorts, movings-away, and short, rear-leg kicks to try and get at the bucket. Smiler managed to deal with them all. Finally, shaken, hot all over, he had the cow stripped and the bucket half full of milk. He carried the bucket well away from Mrs. Brown and then untied her from the tree. Mrs. Brown gave a couple of bucking kicks with her back legs and trotted off to the far end of the pastures.

Smiler went wearily back to the castle lower entrance to be met by the Laird coming out carrying a pail of wet mash for Laggy's pen. He looked down at the short measure of milk in the bucket, then at Smiler, and grinned.

"Kicked the first lot over, did she, lad?"

"Yes, sir – but it was my fault. I didn't have the bucket between my legs like you showed me."

"No matter. She'd have tried something else – like all women. Never been a new lad here that she didn't play up the first time. That idiot of a Willy McAufee she played up for a week. But she'll stand for you tomorrow. Just from the little bit of watching ye I could see you've got good hands. She'll know it, too, and give you no more trouble – unless the mood's on her for some mysterious feminine reason. Right, take the milk up to the dairy, and mind how you go on the stairs. They can be tricky too. Aye –" he grinned broadly "– there's no a stone stairway in the place that at some time or other hasn't claimed the broken neck of a servant or an Elphinstone in the past. And hurry back down. We're not a quarter done yet."

Smiler started up the long stone stairway thinking

that after Mrs. Brown he felt as though he were completely done. He only hoped the Laird was right and that she would stand for him tomorrow. As for today, he wanted no more trouble.

But it was a wish not to be granted. Sitting at the top of the stairs, his back to Smiler, was Midas the golden labrador. Coming up behind him Smiler forgot all about the warning cough with the result that, as he came abreast of the dog, Midas turned and snapped at him.

Smiler jumped to one side to avoid being bitten and the milk pail hit the stone wall, tilted, and half the contents went slipping down the stairs before Smiler could steady the bucket. He groaned aloud as he watched the milky flood cascade over the grey worn stone steps. It was little consolation that Midas, in apology, came up and licked his milky wet hand on the bucket handle.

*　　*　　*

But within a fortnight Smiler was thoroughly at home in the castle and on the island. He knew his way around and never forgot to cough if he came up behind Midas. And with Mrs. Brown, after four or five days during which she tried her usual tricks on him, he became quite confident. Mrs. Brown, deciding that he had served his apprenticeship, now stood quietly for him and there was no need to tie her to the tree. With hands that grew more expert each time Smiler would strip her down. He loved the sound of the warm milk hissing into the bucket and the sweet odour of the beast's flank as he leaned his head against it.

Until he got used to them, and could work out his own system and routine for dealing with them, his daily chores took him a long time. But as he learnt his way around he found himself with more time on his hands than he had expected. Because he liked the Laird so much and was grateful to him he found himself doing something which wild horses couldn't have dragged him to do had he been staying with his Sister Ethel. He actually went around *looking for jobs!*

The main job was the state of the castle. He found dusters and brooms, scrubbing brushes and scourers, and soap and polish, and attacked the place, starting first with the great main room and the wide stairway. He polished and scrubbed and dusted and while he worked he often sang one of his father's songs.

Once the Laird came and watched him and said, smiling, "Samuel M., you'll soon have the place so tidy and spruce that it'll no be a fit abode for a couple of bachelors like ourselves."

"But I like doing it, sir," said Smiler.

"You're sure, lad?"

"Yes, sir."

"That's good then. At first I thought you must be sickening for something."

But although Smiler was happy from being able to please the Laird, there were other things that made him happy before the first week was over. One was the afternoon when he was trying to get the rust off the suit of armour by the terrace door with some wire wool. As he worked away one of the white fantails came sailing through the doorway and perched on his shoulder. Smiler stopped working, delighted, but afraid to move lest the bird take off. But the fantail gave a few slow coos and settled down and slowly Smiler began to work again. After that the other birds and animals began to take to him. Within no time at all he was walking around the place almost as decorated with birds and animals as the Laird himself – and always, wherever he went, Bacon was with him showing no jealousy of the other animals.

But the part of the day that he liked best was after he and the Laird had had their supper in the kitchen. They would wash up together and then, since the evenings were light until very late, they would go down to the beach where a small black and white rowing boat was pulled up and the Laird would take him out on the loch.

He taught Smiler how to row and he taught Smiler how to fly-fish – for the Laird was incapable of getting into a boat without taking a fly rod with him. But this was different fishing from any Joe Ringer or his father had done. The Laird fly-fished while Smiler at the oars kept the boat on a steady drift across the mouth of the small bay. Smiler was fascinated by the man's skill, watching the smooth bend of the rod and the sweet curl of the line as the Laird cast, then let his team of flies sink a little before he began to work them back to the boat. The Laird never caught more than would meet their own and the animals' needs for food. There were small red-and-yellow spotted brown trout and then the larger finnoch, or young sea-trout, which were a steely blue with blackish markings. While the Laird fished he talked and answered Smiler's questions, explaining how the trout and the finnoch were really the same family, only the finnoch had taken it into their heads to migrate out to the sea estuaries each year and then came back to spawn in the burns that ran into the loch. And after fishing, he often sat Smiler with him at his small fly-tying desk in the study off the main hall. He showed him how to dress the flies on the bare hooks, using feathers, coloured silks, gold and silver tinsel wire, and little hackle feathers from the capes of some of the cocks and hens that lived in the poultry run. He taught him, too, the names of the flies, names that are a litany to any fly-fisherman . . . Peter Ross, March Brown, Mallard and Claret, Alexandra, Butcher, Grouse and Orange, Woodcock and Green, Watson's Fancy, Snipe and Purple, Waterhen Bloa . . . hundreds of them. One – the Parmachene Belle – tied with a strip of white duck or swan wing with a slip of red feather alongside it to make it look like a piece of streaky bacon – was so fashioned because the old loggers in Canada and America had used bacon for fishing but – when bacon ran short – they had made flies to imitate it. Smiler's first efforts to tie flies were, as the Laird said, "Enough to put the fear of the Lord into a finnoch and send him off his food for a week." But Smiler, who had good hands, and didn't like to be beaten, persevered and in the end began to tie a very nice fly.

Sometimes while they were fishing, Dobby, the otter with a missing foot that roamed free around the island now, would swim out and circle the boat and get cursed for putting the fish down. But later, when Smiler began to take the boat out by himself, he loved Dobby to come. He would drop the large rock that served as anchor overboard, strip off, and dive into the water and be delighted to see Dobby make circles around him, a stream of silvery bubbles wobbling surfacewards from his nostrils.

Lying in his bed at the end of the third week, curtains drawn to show the light sky of the summer night, Smiler told himself, "Samuel M., if you don't know how lucky you are to get a place like this then you ought to be. You got a good job and you're getting to know things. Like handlin' a boat, and fishing, and all those flies you can make, and the animals and birds. Why it's kind of . . . well, perfect. Not a fly in the ointment" he chuckled to himself— "– except ones you can fish with."

He lay back, feeling Bacon stir at the bottom of the bed, and the thought suddenly struck him. When he found his father in October and things were sorted out, maybe the Laird would let him bring his father up here for the rest of his leave. They could all be together. Gosh! That would be perfect.

*   *   *

The next morning early, as Smiler came back from doing his feeding and cleaning rounds, he looked up to see the flag of St. Andrew flying from one of the corner towers of the castle, lazily flipping its folds in a warm westerly breeze.

As he was making breakfast, keeping an eye on the frying trout and the toast under the grill, the Laird came into the kitchen.

Smiler gave him good morning and then said, "Sir, please, why is the flag flying today?"

"Because, lad," said the Laird, "we want some more supplies, and also I need my newspapers and mail. It's for Mistress Laura to come up."

"But she can't see it right down the other end of the loch, can she?"

"No, she can't. But someone on the hill or the loch will see it and pass the message. You think you're living up here lost like Robinson Crusoe, but ye're not, Samuel M. The hills, the braes and the glens are full of eyes. There's always a keeper, farmer or shepherd to spot the flag and pass the word. And remember this – if there's ever trouble up here all that needs to be done is to fly the flag at half-mast and there'll be someone along within the day."

After breakfast Smiler went down to release Laggy from his pen. The bird was recovering well and each day now he was let out so that he could graze on the grass of the meadow above the small bay, and swim in the water. The gander had got to know Smiler well. Wing still bandaged tightly to its side, Laggy would follow him down to the water and join the other wild fowl that were paddling about in the shallows.

Smiler, seeing the flag flying over the grey towers of the castle, found himself thinking about Laura. Not that he had much time for girls. But it was nice to know she was coming up. She was a bit bossy, of course, and a chatterbox. Still, if a chap, say, had to be cast away on an island with a girl then she'd be better than most. She wouldn't go all helpless and be a nuisance. If he had to choose between his Sister Ethel and Laura he knew which he would choose. Suddenly the thought of being cast away on a desert island with his sister made him go off into a fit of giggles. . . . She'd want everything spick and span, grumbling about footmarks on her nice sandy beach, sweeping around with big palm leaves, and forever scouring away at the tin cans they would use for cooking. Oh, couldn't he just see it! No, thank you. Give him someone like Laura any day.

Laura arrived an hour before noon the next day. Smiler was up in the wood at the back of the castle chopping down some young pine growths to make stakes for an enlargement to the wild-fowl enclosure that the Laird was planning. It was hard work. Not for the first time, he dropped his axe and, with Bacon at his heels, moved quietly to the edge of the rockface drop and lay looking down at the place where the big salmon had its lie behind the under-water boulder. He liked watching it. Mostly the fish rested almost motionless behind the boulder. But now and then, as though bored with its long wait for the autumn floods that would let it run the burn where it would find a spawning mate, it moved off majestically in a slow circle. Watching it, Smiler wondered what it would be like to have a fish that size on his line. In the Laird's study was a stuffed salmon weighing thirty pounds which the Laird had caught years and years before. . . . Thirty pounds, thought Smiler – the line would fair go whizzing out, burn your fingers if you let it. . . . He looked up, the sound of a motor coming to his ears. On the sun dazzle far down the loch he saw the black shape of a boat.

Forgetting his work, he jumped to his feet and began to run back to the castle to tell the Laird that Laura was coming.

The two of them, with an accompaniment of animals and birds, met her at the jetty steps. She was wearing her tam o'shanter and dressed as before.

Smiler leaned over and took the bow rope and made it fast. The boat was more heavily loaded this time with sacks of stores and two butane gas containers. At her feet was a wickerwork hamper which she lifted out with her. After they had passed their greetings she explained that the hamper held a red-throated diver with a broken leg and a young cormorant whose plumage was covered in oil.

The Laird said, "Take them along to the surgery pen, lad. I'll deal with them after lunch."

When Smiler got back from putting the birds in the surgery pen, it was to find Laura in the kitchen getting the lunch trays. She grinned at him and said, "Well, Samuel Miles, I'll say this for you – you keep the kitchen a sight tidier than that daft Willy McAufee used to. And the Laird tells me you're a dab hand with the floor polish and the scrubbing brush. The next time I come up I'll bring you a pretty apron to tie around your waist."

"Don't you . . . well, don't you just dare," said Smiler embarrassed.

"There's no call to be upset," said Laura. "On a farm or a place like this there's no such thing as a man's or woman's work. Just work. You like it here?"

"Of course I do. It's the best job I've ever had," said Smiler.

"And how many jobs have you had in your long life?"

Smiler smiled, suddenly untouched by her teasing, and said, "More than you think."

"Well, here's another for you." She handed him a full tray. "Carry that through to the Laird and I'll bring ours."

They all had lunch in the sunshine on the terrace and during it Laura brought the Laird up to date with all the local news and gossip. For Smiler, listening, none of it made much sense because he knew none of the people or places mentioned. But he was content to sit and listen, feeling that he was beginning to belong to this place and that he would be safe here until October came when he could go to meet his father in Greenock.

After lunch the Laird went off to the surgery to deal with the new invalids and Smiler helped Laura to unship the rest of the stores and stuff from the boat and carry them into the castle. This done, he left Laura in the castle and went off to do his after-noon tasks and to milk Mrs. Brown. When he brought the milk back to the kitchen it was to find that Laura had lit the fire in the big old kitchen range. The kitchen was stifling with the heat although the wide window was open.

"What have you lit that for?" asked Smiler.

"What on earth do you think? That old gas thing may be good enough for you two men on your own. But how would I bake a batch of bread on it, leave alone a proper dinner tonight? But it will be another couple of hours before it's ready so I'll take ye up to Cearciseanan and we'll have a swim."

"Keerk what?" asked Smiler.

"Cearciseanan – that's Gaelic for the Hen and Chickens."

"The Hen and Chickens. What are they?"

"You'll see. Come on."

Laura led Smiler down to her boat and a few moments later they were motoring farther up the long arm of the loch. Laura pointed ahead to the three islands in the middle of the loch, explaining that the big one was called the Hen and the two little ones the Chickens. As she ran the boat ashore on the small beach of the Hen, she reached into a locker under the stern seat and tossed a pair of swimming trunks across to Smiler.

"They're my brother's," she explained. "He's bigger than you, but you can draw them tight with the waist string."

They pulled the boat high on to the beach and then Laura began to undress. Smiler didn't know where to look or what to do as she stripped off sweater and shirt and then began to undo her jeans, but to his great relief he soon saw that she was wearing a two-piece bathing dress under her clothes. He looked quickly away from her sun-brown, firm body and then ran up the beach and undressed himself behind a rock. The swimming trunks were much too big for him but the cord through the waist held them firm. When he came out from behind the rock Laura was already in the water.

"Come on," she called. "We'll swim right round the islands."

Smiler waded into the water and joined her and they began to swim around the three islands. It was quite a long way and Smiler had to admit to himself that it wasn't something he would have set out to do himself. He was a fairly strong swimmer but he soon realized that Laura was a stronger one. Curiously enough, instead of feeling jealous about this, he found himself pleased about it. She was a girl who could look after herself and Smiler liked that. Most of the girls he had known in Bristol before they sent him off to approved school couldn't think about anything else but making up their faces or nattering all the time about clothes.

When they had made the circuit of the islands, they lay on the beach and let the sun dry them.

Laura said, "You really do like it up here with the Laird, don't you, Sammy?"

"Yes, I do," said Smiler. "I like him and I like the place and all the animals and birds. It's like . . ."

"Like what?"

For a moment Smiler didn't reply. His eyes were on the steep cliff face on the far side of the loch, on the purpling heather slopes of the hills above, the green tree-filled cleft of a glen, and the thin white scar of a waterfall marking the higher reaches of a burn. Below the tops was the slow movement of grazing sheep and on the tops now, although he couldn't see them, Smiler knew the red deer would be feeding, their calves hidden in the bracken and tall grasses and heather of the corries. High over the water a pair of buzzards circled and clear across the loch came the sweet, rippling call of sandpipers.

"Well . . ." said Smiler a bit embarrassed, ". . . sort of like . . . well, like paradise."

Laura rolled over and rested on one elbow and smiled at him. "So it might seem. But there's more than that to it. Aye, it's beautiful and it looks good. But there's other things not so good. There's the hoodies always ready to attack some injured creature, there's the golden eagles after a mountain hare for their young, the vixen hunting for her cubs, the wild cat after the grouse and the otters after the fish. Also it's summer now, but you should see it in winter when the hill is all snow and life is hard for beast and man. You're like all summer tourists. All you see is a nice picture postcard sort of place –"

"I'm no tourist!"

"Then what are you?"

"Well . . . I'm a . . . well, I'm a worker."

"Why up here – this isn't your country?"

Smiler said nothing. For the moment he felt very angry with her. Just because this was her country didn't mean that no one else could like it or understand it. He knew, too, that everything in nature had to hunt to live. That was the way it was. And, of course, he knew things were hard in winter.

Suddenly Laura laughed. "You should see your face! It's gone just like my father's does when he's crossed. I was only teasing you." She stood up, the wind taking her dark brown hair as she brushed sand from her legs and arms.

Smiler, his anger suddenly gone, said before he could stop himself, "You like doing that, don't you? Teasin' people."

Laura smiled and pushed her hair back over her neck. "Of course I do, you daft loon – but only those I like. Come on." She turned and ran for the boat.

Smiler stood looking after her and slowly a broad smile flushed across his sun-tanned, freckled face and he had a feeling inside him as though . . . well, as though he had drunk too much fizzy lemonade or something and that he was gradually filling with bubbles that would float him away.

*　　*　　*

As they made their way back to the castle in the boat,

Laura and Smiler were watched from the far southern shores of the loch.

High up on the side of the brae that flanked the burn which ran down from the waterfall, a man was sitting in the shadow of a large boulder at the side of a narrow track holding a pair of field glasses to his eyes. He was a man of about forty, plumpish and heavily built. He wore a brown corduroy jacket, dark breeches and stockings, and heavy walking boots. A rucksack lay on the ground at his side. His face was running with sweat and every now and then he brushed at the cloud of flies that swarmed over his head which was bald with little tufty patches of fair hair above his ears.

He watched Laura and Smiler motor back to the castle and tie the boat up at the jetty. When they disappeared into the castle, he swung the glasses and picked up the figure of the Laird who was digging a hole for one of the posts of the new extension to the wild-fowl enclosure. He watched the Laird for some time and then slowly swung the glasses to make a close survey of the beach and the meadow and the tree-clad rise behind the castle. Then he put the glasses down, rubbed his chin thoughtfully, and began to hum gently to himself as though he were well content. He had a pleasant, round jolly sort of face – except for his eyes which, instead of being jolly and friendly, were still, and cold-looking like marbles.

He fished in his rucksack, took out a can of beer and opened it. He drank from the can, finishing it in two long swallows. He threw the empty can away into the heather and then slowly said aloud to himself, "Billy Morgan, given the right timing, I think you might be on to a bit of all right here. Yes, Billy, something really good. Sweet and easy as kiss your hand."

Five minutes later he was making his way back along the track and a bend in the glenside soon hid him from the sight of the loch.

6

∽ *The Birthday Present* ∽

That evening was one of the nicest that Smiler could remember for a long time. They had dinner in the main hall and Smiler had to admit that, compared with Laura's, his cooking was very rough and ready. They began with smoked trout from the loch and then there was roast chicken – served by the Laird at the head of the table with a great flourishing of carving knife and fork – with roast potatoes and fresh green beans from the small garden patch on the slope above the castle. Afterwards there was blackberry pie (the berries preserved from the previous year's crop) and custard. By the time they were finished Smiler was so full he could hardly move. And, while they ate, the dogs and animals moved around them and a row of fantails and other birds sat on the terrace balustrade outside the open doors and watched them like an audience. Laura had prepared the meal in the two hours since they had come back from swimming.

But when she brought the dinner in Smiler saw, too, that she had found time to change. Her long, brown hair was tied back with a green silk strip and she wore a short red dress with green stripes, and thick-heeled black shoes that went *clack*, *clack* across the polished floor boards. Suddenly she seemed very grown up and different. So much so that Smiler couldn't keep his eyes off her as she carried the dish of chicken to the table – until she said, "And which,

Sammy, would you be gawping at? Me or the chicken?"

It was during the dinner that Smiler learnt something of the history of the Elphinstones and their castle. While he and Laura drank milk and orange juice, the Laird was treating himself to a small bottle of wine. From the moment he had said grace, he kept up an easy flow of talk, telling stories and making them laugh. But the story that Smiler liked best, although it didn't make him laugh, was one about another Sir Alec Elphinstone – an ancestor of the Laird's – whose picture hung at the top of the great stairway. Smiler, who was very fond of history, listened fascinated because the man the Laird was talking about had once lived in this castle, had eaten at the very same table and had fished and swum in the loch outside.

When Charles Edward Stuart – Bonnie Prince Charlie – the grandson of James II, had come back to Scotland to make a bid for the throne of England in 1745, he had landed on the coast not far away and had called all the clansmen to him at Glenfinnan. This was the town to which the truck driver had given Smiler and Bacon a lift from Fort William. The Laird of those days had joined him. He had marched south with the clans to take part in the great victory of Prestonpans, and had soldiered and campaigned with the Prince as far south as Derby where the tide of fortune had turned against Bonnie Prince Charlie.

Finally, retreating into the Highlands, the Prince's forces had been defeated by the Duke of Cumberland, Butcher Cumberland, at Culloden Moor not far from Inverness. After many adventures Bonnie Prince

94

Charlie had escaped the country never to return. With him had gone the Sir Alec Elphinstone of those days, after making a hurried visit to the castle to say goodbye to his wife and children.

The Laird said, "Aye, he went with his Prince. And, like him, never to return. From those days the House of Elphinstone has never recovered. The Butcher's men sacked the castle of every valuable except a few pieces of silver plate that Lady Elphinstone hid. But the one thing they wanted and didn't get was the Elphinstone jewels. Sir Alec took them with him, they say, to raise further funds for the Prince. We've been poor as cathedral mice ever since. When you go up to bed, Samuel M., you can see the jewels. Next to Sir Alec's picture at the top of the stairs is a painting of his wife. A grand lady and she is wearing some of the jewels."

"What would you do with them, if you had them now, sir?" asked Smiler.

"Do? Why, laddie, be sensible and sell the lot, and use the money to good purpose. Put the farms in order, plant the forest, break new land, and polish up this old ruin and leave a fine going concern for my son. But most of all – for there would be money to spare – I'd set up a fine wild life sanctuary at this end of the loch. Turn it over to the beasts and the birds. Aye, and have enough money still to pay for wardens to keep people's thieving hands off the beasts. The sea ospreys would come back and breed in peace from egg stealers, and so would the golden eagles, the peregrines, the merlins and hobbies, and that bonnie bird the hen harrier. When I was a boy there were always two pairs of ospreys breeding here. One on the Hen and the other pair on the far Chicken.

And I'd have a surgery and hospital and maybe a wee experimental station for studying. We all have dreams, laddie, and that's mine. And dream it will stay." He looked at them both and slowly smiled. "Of course, I wouldn't forget my friends. I'd buy Mistress Laura here a good farm and leave her to find a fine, hard-working young man to go with it."

"And what would you buy Samuel?" asked Laura.

The Laird turned to Smiler. "What would I buy you, Samuel M.?"

Embarrassed for the moment, Smiler said, "I don't know, sir."

"Then you should do," said Laura. "You're old enough to begin thinking about the future. What about –" she grinned "– since you're so taken with cooking and housework – a hotel?"

"I don't want nothing to do with any hotel, thank you. I want to be outside with animals and things. Perhaps, well . . . perhaps I'd like to be a farmer, or someone like –"

"Like what?" asked the Laird.

"Well, like a vet. So I could look after animals like you do, sir. Only I'm not very good at learning. And I'd have to get exams and go to University and all that."

"University – that's a waste of time," said Laura. "All they do there is grow long hair and beards and want everything put on a plate before them. You should hear my father about it."

"Take no heed of Mistress Laura," said the Laird. "If you want to do a thing you can find ways. Maybe sometime –" he glanced at Laura slyly "– when we're not plagued with womenfolk – we'll have a chat about it."

"Well, that's aye put me in my place," said Laura. "However, while you're waiting to decide your future, you can help me carry these things back to the kitchen and we'll make the Laird some coffee."

Much later, after they had sat with the Laird having his coffee on the terrace and the birds had gone off to their roosts and purple and grey shadows had claimed the face of the loch and the night sky had turned to a wash of silver light with the stars studding it like gems, Smiler took his candlestick off the main hall table and went up to bed.

At the top of the stairs he held the candle up to throw light on the portraits of Sir Alec Elphinstone and his wife. Sir Alec he had studied before. He was the man holding a sword and buckler. But Lady Elphinstone Smiler had never properly looked at. She was sitting on a red velvet chair in the main hall. Behind her, through the open terrace door, could be seen the sun sparkle on the loch and the distant outline of the Hen and Chickens and the far hills. She wore a tall, white wig with elaborate ringlets falling to her bare shoulders. Her long dress was of grey silk with ruchings of blue ribbons at the neck, sleeves and skirt-hem. One of her hands rested on the head of a black greyhound. On her fingers were three rings set with great sparkling stones which Smiler imagined must be diamonds. About her throat and looping over her bosom was a long necklace of green stones which Smiler guessed could be emeralds. On the fingers of her other hand which grasped a tall, elaborately mounted shepherd's crook, were more rings. But the most splendid of all the jewellery she wore was on a black velvet band that ran across her high forehead and was caught back under her wig.

It was shaped in an eight-pointed star. The centre of the star was an oval stone of a bluish colour, shot with purple and green fire, and each ray of the star was studded with diamonds and pearls. The whole thing, even in the dim candlelight, blazed in a great burst of rippling colours.

Gosh! thought Smiler. Just fancy what all that lot would have been worth! A fortune. And, although he could understand why the long dead Sir Alec had felt he wanted to go off and support his Prince, he couldn't help feeling, too, that it was a shame that the Laird didn't have the jewels now. Fighting and battles and putting people back on their thrones was important of course in those days. But today . . . well, the Laird could have done more good with the money they would fetch. Just fancy, if there were sea ospreys nesting on the Hen right now, coming down, wings up-folded, legs and talons thrust out to take the trout from the loch for their young.

From behind him, where she had come silently up the stairs, Laura said, making him jump, "How much longer are you going to stand there mooning at her?"

Smiler, recovering from his surprise, said, "I was really lookin' at the jewels. But she's very . . . well, beautiful, isn't she?"

"Aye," said Laura judiciously, "she is. Though she'd have had trouble doing the cooking and house-work in that wig and fancy dress."

Used now to Laura's sharp comments, Smiler grinned and said, "Anyway, I bet you'd like to dress up like that if you could."

"Perhaps I would if I was going to a fancy dress ball."

As they climbed the stairways and threaded the stone corridors to their rooms, Smiler asked, "Is the Laird so very badly off?"

"Aye, by his lights he is, and that's what counts. But he's no so poor as any farmer or fisherman. Did you really mean that about wanting to be a vet?"

"I don't know," said Smiler. "I suppose so – but I got a lot to do first before I can think about it."

Laura paused at the door of her room. "Like what?" she asked.

"Well . . . things."

"You've told the Laird about these . . things?"

"Yes."

"And you can't tell me?"

"Perhaps . . . sometime."

"I'd like you to, sometime. Goodnight, Sammy." She gave him a smile and went into her room.

*   *   *

Laura stayed the next day and night and then went back. The Laird and Smiler were on their own again. For Smiler the days went by like a dream. He worked hard, looking after the animals and clearing up the castle rooms as best he could. Even so, he found that he had a lot of spare time on his hands. By now he knew every bird and beast about the place and they all knew him. Wherever he went or worked there was always one or another of them with him as well as Bacon. But there were two animals which had taken a particular liking to him. One was Laggy who, by now, was growing fat with good and regular food. The greylag would waddle alongside of him, wing still bandaged to its side. In the evenings when he

99

went out in the boat to fish it would swim behind. When he hooked a trout some of the excitement of the catch seemed to pass to it and it would raise its long neck skywards and cry *gag-gag-gag* as though applauding the catch. The other animal was the otter, Dobby. From the Laird Smiler knew now that the otter was so called from the Gaelic word for otter – Dobhran. Laggy would never follow Smiler beyond the limits of the small bay, but Dobby did not mind how far they went.

On the still evenings, when there was only the occasional breath of a breeze, Smiler liked to let the boat drift down the far side of the island towards the spot where the big salmon had its lie. There had been no rain for weeks now. The level of the loch was dropping fast and the water, though it always held a faint umber stain of peat, was as clear as glass. Smiler would hang over the side of the boat and drift right over the big fish's lie and the salmon would not move until the following shadow of the boat, cast by the westering sun, touched it. Then it would move off slowly. But sometimes it would see Dobby swimming underwater first. Then, with a great sweep of its noble tail, it would be gone leaving a puff of stirred-up sand and gravel rising like a small cloud from its lie. Dobby, Smiler noticed, liked this side of the island, where the water went down deep from the steep cliffs. It was a good place for trout and finnoch. Dobby would roll over lazily on the water and then go under and soon be out of sight. Sometimes he would be underwater for so long that Smiler would become anxious about him, but eventually the otter would surface with his catch and then lie on his back in the water and eat it or swim to a favourite rock at the foot of the cliff and eat there. Once or twice, however, he was down so long that Smiler was sure something had happened to him. On the second occasion he rowed back to the castle jetty almost in a panic to tell the Laird about it. But, as he got out of the boat, Dobby surfaced at the steps and came ashore.

Although he only rowed over twice to the far south shore of the loch, Smiler knew from the talks he had had with the Laird a great deal about the wild life over there, and sometimes the Laird would get out his maps and show Smiler the maze of lochs, burns and hills that stretched away southwards from the loch.

The days and weeks passed and August was running out. The purple of the heather was fading a little and when Smiler walked through it little clouds of pollen rose from it. Up on the hills the roe-deer and red-deer calves were growing fast. Soon it would be autumn and the red-deer would start their rutting, the echoes of the calling stags roaring and rolling through the tops. And soon, Smiler told himself, it would be October and he would be off to meet his father. When the moment came he knew he would be sad to go.

One evening after they had had their supper, the Laird rose to his feet and said, "Samuel M., we've both got a job to do before Mistress Laura comes up on Friday. I'll show you yours – which is not difficult. Though mine may not be possible unless we get some rain or a good stiff breeze on the water. Come with me."

He led the way to the foot of the great oak stairway. The big bottom post was decorated on top with a carved lion holding a shield between its forepaws. Puzzled, Smiler followed him.

"Take the beast's head," said the Laird, "and give it a good twist clockwise."

Smiler did as he was told. As the head turned he noticed that the carved collar about its neck hid the moving joint. There was a faint click and, lower down the big post, one of the small decorated panels flipped open on a spring. Behind the panel was a narrow cavity with a heavy, old-fashioned key in it.

The Laird took it out and shut the panel door. As he did so the lion's head turned back to its original position.

"Gosh, that's very dodgy, isn't it, sir?" said Smiler.

"Dodgy, my lad, is the word," said the Laird. "And dodgy in my ancestors' days they had to be. This castle is full of hiding places. Hiding places for men and women in trouble and for money and the good Lord knows what. This is the key of the antiquated safe in my study."

"Do you always keep the key there, sir?"

"No, Samuel M., I do not. It would not be prudent in a good Scot. I hide it where my fancy takes me."

The Laird led Smiler into his crowded little study where an old-fashioned safe sat on the floor in a corner. It was a big safe, taller than Smiler. The Laird opened the safe and from it he drew out four bundles wrapped in green baize cloth.

He put the bundles on the table and unwrapped them. Smiler's eyes grew round with surprise. There was a pair of eight-branched silver candlesticks, two wide shallow silver bowls, their rims decorated with a running relief of birds and animals and their centres engraved with the arms of the Elphinstone family and two sets of condiment dishes. Reclining mermaids held the salt dishes and there were two leaping salmon with large perforations in their heads through which to shake rough ground pepper. The most magnificent of all was a long, narrow dish, which was supported at each corner by royally antlered red-deer stags rising up on their hind feet. All the silver was dull and tarnished, but the beauty of it made Smiler catch his breath.

As he set it out the Laird explained that the silver was all that was left of the Elphinstone treasure and that it had been a gift from Charles the First to one of his ancestors.

"Crikeys, sir," said Smiler. "It must be worth an awful lot of money."

"A fair bit, Samuel M. A fair bit, laddie. And many's the time I've thought of selling it. But it canna be done. 'Twas the personal gift of a king. Also, there's a saying that if it ever leaves the castle for good then the last of the Elphinstones goes with it. Personally, being a rational man, I doubt it, but like a good Elphinstone –" his bright blue eyes twinkled and he scratched at his beard "– I'm in no mind to take any chances. Anyway, there's your job. You have the key and you know where it lives and it has to be cleaned by this weekend. Aye, lad, it must shine so bright that your eyes will blink to see it. With this drought going and the loch like a sheet of glass you've got the easier job."

"What is your job, sir?"

"To fill the big dish there, lad. What good is it without a royal fish to grace it?"

"You mean a salmon, sir?"

The Laird gave Smiler a mock serious look and said, "Samuel M., learn one thing fast. When a good Scot or a good fisherman talks of a *fish*, only one thing is meant. A salmon. And for this occasion there never has been a fish lacking."

"But what is the occasion, sir?"

"Can ye not guess? The silver, the fish, Mistress Laura coming on Friday and the rest of her family and a few others on the Saturday. A real ceilidh – and one that happens only once a year."

"I know," said Smiler quickly, "it's your birthday, sir."

"Aye, it is, Samuel M."

Before he could stop himself Smiler said, "And will you be very old, sir?"

The Laird grinned and then said, "Old enough to want to do better, lad, and young enough to keep on trying – which makes me somewhere between one and one hundred. Now then, I'm away on my own to try for a fish before the light goes."

But when the Laird came back as the last light went he brought no salmon. The next morning, when his round of work was finished, Smiler took one of the silver candelabra into the kitchen and sat in the sunshine at the window and began his polishing. The cat and her kittens were on the long seat beside him. Bacon was curled up in a patch of sun on the floor and Midas was lying full stretch across the open doorway. The small yellow-brown bird which Smiler had first seen perching on the Laird's sporran came and sat on the window ledge. Smiler knew now that it was a siskin which had suffered from a bad infection that the Laird had cured.

Smiler polished and polished as though his life depended on it. Because he liked the Laird so much he wanted the silver for this birthday to be brighter than it had ever been before. Also, as he worked, he considered the problem of money. He was a practical, straightforward thinker and he liked to have a problem to work on. He knew by now all the things the Laird would like to do on his estates and also for the animals and birds which he treated. If he were the Laird and wanted all that . . . well, he wondered what he would do about the silver? It was nice to have, of course – and it was a present from a king. But, gosh – it would sell for enough money to do some of the things. Still, it was a kind of family thing. Like the big silver watch his father always carried. That had belonged to his father's great-grandfather and, although it had long stopped going, he knew nothing would ever make his father part with it – and there had been hard times in the past when even a few pounds would have helped. It was a kind of good luck thing. And so was the silver, too. And you didn't sell your good luck.

When they were having their lunch on the terrace, the sun beating down on the still loch, making the Hen and Chickens dance gently in a heat haze across the water, he asked the Laird:

"You wouldn't ever sell the silver, sir, I know. But then – why did you say you would sell the jewels if you had them?"

"A good question, lad. A gift is one thing. But a handful of jewels bought by the family out of its wealth in the past – they're just possessions. And as a family's fortunes go up and down, so they buy or sell. Some of my land I've sold to put the money to good use on the estate. And the jewels I'd sell for the same reason. They came from and belong to the Elphinstones and every head of the house has a right to make his own decision about them. But it is also an idle question, lad. The jewels have long ago departed. The big question now is – when am I going to get a fish?"

That afternoon the Laird and Smiler took Laggy into the surgery. The Laird had decided that the wing had had long enough to set. The bandages were cut away and the splints removed. Laggy squatted docilely in Smiler's hands while this was done. The Laird examined the wing, his long, capable fingers probing and pressing carefully.

"As good as new," he said. "He'll be flying within the week. But first he's got a lot of preening and oiling of the wing to do before he'll feel like taking to the air."

Smiler carried Laggy outside and set him down. For a while the gander just stood still, unused to the freedom of its left wing. Then it gave itself a little shake and followed Smiler down to the water's edge. Smiler watched it paddle out into the shallows. Floating in the slow current drift Laggy began to preen and sort the long primaries and the secondaries of its left wing flight-feathers. It gave Smiler a good feeling to watch the gander. After all, if it hadn't been for himself and Bacon the greylag wouldn't have been sitting on the water as right as rain again. That was a good thing to see. Probably that's what a vet was nearly always feeling. Feeling good because he had put some animal right. He sighed suddenly. Blimey, it was still a long way to October, and then there would be everything to be sorted out by his

Dad, and then. . . . How could he ever get to be a vet? He'd have to go back to school, or something, again. And all that studying! And, anyway, his father wouldn't be able to afford things like college and so on. He grinned to himself suddenly – not even selling great-grandfather's ropey old silver watch would help!

*　　*　　*

During the next three days the Laird fished early morning and late evening for his birthday fish without any success. All day the sun was a brazen orb in a cloudless sky, and the loch was a great sheet of tinted glass with only now and then the breath mark of a feeble, fast-dying zephyr to flaw it. From time to time during the day Smiler would see the Laird straighten up from whatever work he was doing, raise his eyes to the sky and say, "Oh Lord – if it's no great inconvenience to you, please send a roistering south-westerly with rain in it!" But the good Lord showed no signs of being willing to oblige.

Smiler's interest, apart from polishing the silver every day, which he did in order to keep it bright, was in Laggy. Watching the gander on the bay he would sometimes see the bird half-raise himself in the water and flap both of his wings. But he never did it with any great effort. It was almost, Smiler thought, as though the gander wasn't ready yet to trust the mended left wing for flying.

On the Friday morning Laura arrived just before lunch. The boat was heavily laden with supplies which Smiler helped her to carry up to the castle.

While they were having lunch together in the

kitchen Laura said, "Of course you've thought up a birthday present for the Laird?" One look at Smiler's face told her that he hadn't. She raised her eyebrows in despair. "You men! You're all the same. My father, now, never remembers for my mother until the last minute and then he dashes into Mallaig or Fort William and pays a lot of money for something she doesn't want."

On the spur of the moment Smiler said, "Well, I did think I'd make up a special fly and tie it for him."

Laura tossed her hair back and said sharply, "And that's something you've just thought of, Sammy, and you know it. Anyway, if it's a fly that can catch a fish in these conditions, he should have it now or I can see him going without his birthday fish for the first time for years. You'd better put your thinking cap on and decide on something for him."

A little cross with her and himself, Smiler stood up and said, "You don't have to worry. I'll think of something."

He went off to do his early afternoon jobs, cleaning out pens, cutting more stakes for the wild-fowl enclosure, and milking Mrs. Brown. All the time he worked, he was wondering what he could give the Laird. What on earth could he give him? There weren't any shops around. He *could* have tied him a special fly if Laura hadn't been so scoffing about that. Often these days when the darkness drew in he would light the oil lamp in the Laird's study and sit at the bench tying a fly. He had become reasonably expert with the simpler ones. But salmon flies, he knew, were big, complicated affairs and very difficult to tie. One evening, working at the desk, he had remembered what the Laird had told him about the Parmachene Belle being fashioned after streaky bacon. Bacon was his dog. He had thought that if his dog, in a way, had a fly called after him, it would be nice if he had a fly called after himself. A Smiler fly. So he had set to and invented a Smiler fly, chuckling to himself as he had worked at it because he had used only colours that had something to do with himself. He had made the tail from a few wisps of fibre from a cock pheasant's tail – because the feather was sort of freckled like himself. The body had been easy. He just wound on yellow silk for his own fair hair. For the little throat hackle under the body of the fly he had used a tiny scrap of jay's feather because it was blue like his eyes. For the wings he had used two small slips from grey goose quill feathers – because it was through Laggy that he had come to the castle. But although he had used the fly once or twice he had never caught anything on it. Most likely, he felt, because the hook was a bit big for trout or finnoch to fancy in such hot weather and low water conditions. Anyway, he couldn't tie a special fly for the Laird now. Laura had made that impossible. There were times, he told himself, when he could give that girl a good thump! Would have done had she been a boy.

The thought of the present worried him all the afternoon. In the end he decided that the best he could do was to make a birthday card for the Laird. He was a fair hand at drawing and printing. He would get some stuff from the study tonight and take it up to his room when he went to bed and work on it quietly.

When he got back to the castle later that afternoon

it was to be met by Laura whose face was red and hot-looking. She said, "That kitchen's roasting with the range on. I'll do the rest of the baking for the party when it's cooler tonight. Let's go down to the Hen and have a swim."

So Smiler rowed them down to the Hen, beached the boat, and they had a swim. Then they got back into the boat and Laura lazed in the stern while Smiler sat up forward. There was no need for either of them to row because the loch current set in a gentle drift westwards back to Elphinstone castle. Smiler, who didn't like sitting and doing nothing, picked up the fly rod which now – like the Laird – he always carried in the boat. It was an old split cane rod which the Laird had handed to him for his own special use, saying, "It's called a 'Knockabout', Samuel M. But if I ever see you knock it about I'll put you on bread and water for a week."

With Laura half asleep in the stern, Smiler flicked his line and cast out ahead as they drifted. Then, as the Laird had taught him, he began to work his flies back just fast enough to beat the drift of the boat. He was using two flies, one on the tail of the nylon cast which sank quite deep and another, a dropper, much higher up the cast. Smiler liked to work the rod and line so that the dropper just came tripping and bobbing along the water surface. Mostly, he had noticed, he got trout and finnoch to the dropper more than to the tail fly.

From behind him as he began to fish, Laura said sleepily, "You dafty, you'll never get a fish on a day like this. The trout have more sense than to come up and risk sunburn. They're all tucked away, cool and easy, in the shade at the bottom."

Smiler said nothing. All right, he might not get a fish – in fact was pretty certain that he wouldn't – but he just liked the ritual of fishing. He liked the sweet action of casting and seeing the two flies drop gently to the surface.

And, anyway, you never knew. If he was daft enough to be fishing, then there might be a fish daft enough to come to his fly. How often had he heard the Laird himself say, "Laddie, if there's one thing for certain about fishing it is that there is nothing certain about it." So sucks to Laura, thought Smiler.

The boat drifted down towards the castle. Behind Smiler, Laura went to sleep. As they neared the little bay, Smiler saw Laggy swimming near the shallows and he wondered when the gander would fly again. It had been so long since Laggy had flown that Smiler wondered if the bird had forgotten how to do it. What a stupid idea, he told himself. One day Laggy would take off.

Normally, when they were abreast of the bay, Smiler would have taken the oars and pulled in to the jetty, but today it was so much cooler on the water that he let the boat drift on into the shadow cast by the tall cliff face of the island. Looking at the rocks some twenty yards away on his right he could see how much the loch had dropped in the last weeks. He reckoned it was a good four feet already. The big boulder at the foot of the cliff which was Dobby's favourite place for eating fish was now high and dry.

As Smiler's eyes came back from Dobby's boulder, his right arm moved automatically sending the line and cast out ahead of him. The flies dropped gently to the smooth surface and he watched the slight ripple die as the tail fly sank. Gently he began to work the line in and lifted the tip of the rod to bring the dropper tripping on the surface. The fly had dapped along no more than a couple of feet when Smiler saw something which he had never seen before in his life.

A great head and a curving length of smooth, dark, steely back broke water like a porpoise surfacing. The whole action was so lazy and slow that it seemed to go on for ages; seemed in fact to Smiler that it wasn't happening, that he was imagining it, that it was all a warm, lazy daydream.

A few seconds later, though, he knew that it was no dream. The head and tailing fish sank out of sight. Almost immediately there was a hard tug as the dropper fly was taken, and line began to scream off Smiler's reel.

Smiler sat and held the curving rod and wondered what on earth he was supposed to do. His heart began to pound wildly with excitement. Then, when Smiler felt that all the line must be off the reel, the wild, first run of the fish stopped. The line went slack and the rod straightened.

It was at this moment that the boat rocked a little and Laura, her voice calm, spoke from behind him. "You're into a fish, Sammy. Wind in the slack quickly and get in touch with him – if he's still there."

Hardly knowing that he was obeying her, Smiler began to wind line back as fast as he could. He got about ten yards in when he felt the pressure of the fish on the line and the rod bent again.

Behind him Laura said quietly, "Easy now. Keep your head. Make *him* do the work. If he wants to run let him, but the moment he stops – get in touch again. And don't worry about him taking all your line. I'll see to that, or my name's not the same as my father's."

Deep down in the water, twenty yards from the boat, the fish tugged hard and then began to run again. This time Smiler, coming more to grips with the situation, let him have the line but held the rod tip up so that the fish had to work against its gentle but insistent power. Once, thinking to steady the fast run, Smiler put his hand down to try and brake the revolving face of the reel, but the spinning handle smacked his fingers sharply, drawing blood from them. From behind him Laura, now on the centre-thwart and unshipping the oars, yelled, "Don't do that, you loon. He'll break you!"

The fish took thirty yards of line and bored deep. Suddenly, the strain went off rod and line. This time Smiler, beginning to be steadier now, reeled in until he made contact. But the moment he did he put no great pressure on the fish. He just held the rod so that he could feel the fish at the other end and the fish could feel him, and he said aloud, "Holy Crikeys! What am I going to do?"

Laura, the oars out now and gently paddling, looked over her shoulder and said, "You're going to do what I tell ye, Sammy, and if you do you'll have the finest birthday present the Laird could wish for. But if ye don't then ye'll have lost the first salmon you ever got into. What's the breaking strain of your cast?"

Now, from his father and Joe Ringer in the past, and from the Laird since he had been at the castle, Smiler knew all about the breaking strains of nylon – and he knew exactly what his was.

He said dismally, "It's only five pounds."

Very calmly Laura said, "That's aye fine for a big trout. But yon's a handsome fish. You've got to treat him like a baby, nice and easy. And don't think it's going to be a quick business – because it isn't. And sooner or later, when he jumps, and jump he will, lower your rod point fast or he may break you and –"

But Smiler didn't hear any more. The line began to sing from the reel again. The rod point bowed and there was no thought or feeling in Smiler except the deep, agonizing excitement that came from the almost magical contact between himself and the fighting fish.

From behind him Laura, no stranger to this situation, helped him. As the fish ran she rowed hard on the same course and called to Smiler that, whenever he could, he was to take up line, but without using any force that would put too much strain on the thin nylon cast.

So began for Smiler one of the most exhausting, demanding, and exciting thirty minutes of his life. The fish ran, and Smiler gave it line, and Laura rowed after it and they gained line back. The fish ran again and took them well out into the loch, away from the island. Then it lay still, deep down, and Smiler just kept in touch with it, realizing now that each time the fish ran it was tiring itself a bit more. And so far, except for the paralysing moment when the fish had head-and-tailed to take the fly, Smiler had seen no sign of it.

The sulking fish moved unexpectedly and, this time, headed straight back for the boat. The line went slack across the water. Laura, pulling the boat around and away from the line of the run which would have taken it under the keel, shouted instructions at Smiler. He swung the rod out clear from the bows of the boat and reeled in fast. To his relief, in a few seconds he felt the fish again. But no sooner did he feel it than the fish was off, away at an angle back towards the island, and this time it jumped.

Twenty yards from the boat the salmon came out of the water with a sudden explosion of surface spray. It soared upwards in a great flashing curve of silver flank and gleaming yellowy-white underbelly. For a moment or two it hung in the air as though fixed and carved in its power leap for all time.

"Rod tip!" shouted Laura.

But Smiler scarcely heard her. He just stared at the leaping fish, transfixed by the beauty and exciting splendour of the sight – and he forgot to lower his rod tip.

The great fish crashed back into the loch, spray spouting high in the air, a rain of water glinting in the sun, and then was gone from sight. The rod in Smiler's hand straightened and the line running from its tip went still and slack.

Behind him Laura shouted, "You loon – you've lost him!"

And Smiler was sure he had lost the fish. He began to reel in, yard after yard, and there was no sensation of contact at all on the line. A terrible wave of disappointment swamped him. "You fool, you fool, Samuel M.," he lectured himself. "You've lost the Laird's birthday present and the first salmon you've ever hooked!" He turned towards Laura and, long-faced, gave a despondent shrug of his shoulders. He was about to say something to her when the loose line coming back through the rings of the rod suddenly jerked, tautened, and twanged into life. The next moment line was running out faster than it had ever done before.

It was from this moment that Smiler really became a fisherman. He was trembling with excitement, and he had a lot to learn, but there was a resolute, fighting part of him now which kept saying, "Keep your head, Samuel M. Keep your head."

And as far as he could he did keep his head. When the fish ran, he let him go. Then, as Laura rowed after the fish, Smiler took in line and made gentle but firm contact with the salmon. Now and again he could feel the fish give savage tugs with its head to try and free itself from the fly. A few minutes later it jumped again. But this time Smiler was ready for it. He lowered the rod tip and, as he recovered line, felt the fish still on.

For ages, it seemed to Smiler, the fish took them up and down the loch. They went beyond the end of the castle island and then back almost as far as the Hen, and then back until they were off the small bay – and, with each passing minute, Smiler wondered how long he would be able to hold out. His arms and hands ached and under the hot sun he was running with sweat – and it didn't help that every time he made some small mistake Laura shouted a correction to him from her place at the oars and he wished she would shut up. But he had to admit to himself that she knew how to handle the boat, following the fish fast, swinging hard aside when the fish ran for them, and holding it gently in position when the fish halted and sulked far down in the deep water.

It was during one of these lulls in the battle that the fish slowly came up from the depths and rolled briefly on the surface, its belly flashing.

Laura said, "Aye, Sammy, that's the sign. The beast's tiring. Keep your head now and we've got him."

Eyes on the skirl of foam-flecked water where the fish had gone out of sight, Smiler said despairingly, "But how are we going to get him? There's only a small trout net in the boat. That's useless."

"You'll no need a net, Sammy. We'll take him into the bay and beach him. Just you do what I tell you."

So, under Laura's instructions, the operation began. She started to edge the boat beachwards while Smiler gave or took line as the fish followed or moved away. But, minute after minute, the fish was worked slowly towards the beach, and every little while the salmon came to the surface and rolled, showing gleaming flanks and pale belly, and then dived away into a fast but much shorter run.

Suddenly behind him Smiler heard the bows of the boat grate on the gravel of the beach.

Laura said, "Keep your eyes on him. Keep the pressure easy, and step out."

Holding the bending rod high, his eyes out on the water where the fish was, Smiler stepped overboard and almost up to his waist. He waded ashore and, from the corner of his eye, saw Laura jump out and pull the light boat up on to the beach clear of the water.

The next moment she was racing past him down the beach and shouting, "Now bring him in below you and leave it to me. Don't force him. Just baby him. He'll come now."

Gently Smiler began to put strain on the fish. Not much, but enough to show the tired salmon who was master. Slowly the fish obeyed and Smiler won line.

From the beach below him, Laura called, "Watch him. When he sees me waiting he'll make a last run."

And, sure enough, as Smiler shortened line and slowly swung the great fish into the shallow water at the beach edge, the salmon saw Laura. The fish turned and ran and Smiler, in command and clear-headed now, let him go. But the run was short and he worked the fish back until it was held in six inches of water over the gravel slope of the beach. The fish rolled once or twice, struggled briefly, and then was still from exhaustion.

Laura went into the water and slowly around the fish so that it was between her and the shore. She bent down with an easy, confident movement and caught the wrist of the fish's great tail in one strong hand and – each action flowing sweetly into the next – she lifted the salmon high and walked up on to the beach.

Before Smiler could move she dropped the arching, struggling fish to the ground, picked up a large stone, and gave it two quick, expert taps on the head and killed it.

Smiler ran up and stopped, staring down at the fish. It was enormous. It lay there quivering gently, its spotted, steely, silver flanks and belly just touched with the coming rusty red of its spawning colours, long curving underjaw showing it to be a cock fish and – deep set in the scissors of its jaws – the tightly bedded fly which it had taken.

Suddenly a great surge of elation swept over

Smiler and he did two things which, in his calmer moments, he would never have dreamt of doing. He tossed the rod to the ground in a way which would have got him bread and water for a week and then began to dance around the fish, shouting, "We've done it! We've done it!" And then, the second thing, he suddenly grabbed Laura and danced her around with him, hugging her to him and kissing her, and his excitement was so great that it was not until a long time afterwards that he remembered that she had hugged and kissed him back.

* * *

But all victories bring dark moments to the conquering spirit. The fish weighed eighteen pounds when the Laird – full of praise for Smiler – put it on the scales. And there was more jubilation when it was discovered that it had been caught on the Smiler fly. But there was an agony in Smiler during all the jubilation. The moment he could get free, he slipped out of the castle and raced with Bacon up through the woods to the cliff edge overlooking the spot where he had first hooked the salmon. Lying with his head thrust out over the cliff top, he looked down, knowing that, if the salmon he had so often watched was not there, then wild horses could never drag him to eat a mouthful of fish at the birthday party.

To his great relief, the fish was still there, a long dark shadow, lying in the lee of the boulder. Smiler got up, and with Bacon at his heels, went happily back to the castle.

7

✍ *The King of the Castle* ✍

The Laird's birthday party was the best party Smiler had ever known.

The next morning before lunch two large motor boats arrived from the far end of the loch bringing Laura's mother and father and her brother who worked on the farm, and six other people, neighbours and friends of the Laird. In a short while everywhere there was a great laughing and chattering, and joking and to-and-froing, and a climbing up to rooms and down again, and people being lost in the maze of corridors, and a stern warning coming from Laura and her mother that nobody, but nobody, would be welcomed in the kitchen.

The sun blazed down on the loch as though its thirst was so great and lasting that it meant to drain it dry and still not be satisfied. Bacon got excited with so much company and ran in and out of legs and got chased out of the kitchen. Midas lay in the sun across the terrace entrance and, as people passed unwarily, nipped and growled until he got tired with the whole process and went soundly to sleep. And the birds, the fantails and the whole coloured collection of jay, owl, magpie, siskin, sat around on the parapets and window cornices and wondered what was happening. But the wild fowl, a little upset by the confusion, kept well away at the far end of the beach, and Laggy paddled out into the bay and turned his back on the whole affair.

On the terrace Smiler and Laura had set up a long trestle table for lunch. One end was covered with glasses and bottles of beer and whisky and cider and jugs of milk and orange juice – and, while they were all drinking before lunch, Smiler's salmon, yet to be cooked, was brought in on the great silver dish and exhibited. Smiler and Laura had to tell the whole story of its catching and they were bombarded with questions. Smiler, who never meant to part with it as long as he lived, brought the Smiler fly from his pocket and it was handed around and discussed by the men and a note made of its dressing. Laura's father, Jock Mackay, a craggy man with warm brown eyes wreathed in weather wrinkles, declared, "Aye and it must be a bonnie flee that can bring a fish up with the loch as it is." Then he winked at Smiler and added, "And I've no doubt that Laura, here, badgered you with her shouts and instructions. Ye should have been warned that she's a good but noisy ghillie."

When Smiler fairly said, "She was fine, sir. I couldn't have done it without her," Mrs. Mackay, warm-skinned, dark-haired, a big-bodied, handsome woman, said, "There you are, Jock Mackay, there's a lesson in gallantry that all ye men could take to heart."

The Laird, who was wearing his best jacket and kilt and had banished the mice, grass snakes and other occupants from his clothes for the day, went from one to the other, joking and chatting and refusing to be drawn about his age – except to say that he would never see twenty-one again.

In the afternoon while Smiler was in his bedroom, there was a knock on the door and Laura came in carrying a parcel and put it on his bed.

"What's that?" asked Smiler.

"It's a present from my mother."

"A present? What sort of present?"

"If you open it you can see."

Smiler opened the parcel. Inside was a green and white striped shirt, a grey cardigan, a pair of brown trousers with a little white stripe in them, a pair of suede shoes and some green socks.

Before Smiler could say anything Laura went on, "For dinner tonight everyone dresses up. And knowing you had nothing . . . well, Mum thought . . ."

"But I can't . . . I mean, she oughtn't to do this. She doesn't know me."

"Don't be daft. Of course she knows you from me. And don't you tell her that she mustn't do something. That's the quickest way to get a piece of her tongue. Anyway –" she grinned teasingly "– you're the birthday hero. You've got to look your best."

She was gone before Smiler could think of anything to say. But as he looked down at the clothes he had a nice warm feeling about Mrs. Mackay.

When Smiler put on his new clothes and went down to the main hall that evening, he was glad that he had them for everyone had changed to their best clothes. The men were sitting around on the terrace, having their drinks before dinner. One of them was dressed in full Scottish piper's regalia and he was marching up and down the terrace playing on his pipes a selection of laments and marches that went wailing and rolling and skirling out over the quiet waters of the loch.

When the dinner was served Laura came in bearing the great silver dish with the birthday fish on it, led by the piper who headed her twice round the table before the dish was set in place. Everyone clapped and cheered and then rose and was silent as the Laird said grace. Smiler couldn't stop looking at Laura, who was wearing a long white velvet dress with a great sash of Mackay tartan looped over her shoulder and caught at her waist with a silver buckle that held a great cairngorm stone. Suddenly, remembering how he had kissed her on the beach, he lowered his head as he felt his cheeks burn. Gosh, what a thing to do!

But he soon forgot his embarrassment as the dinner got under way and the evening celebrations began. The flames from the candles in their silver holders rose still and golden in the warm night air. The noble fish was served and it melted in Smiler's mouth like cream and caviar. It was followed by a great saddle of lamb and dishes of steaming vegetables. The glasses were filled with wine and a glass was served to Smiler – but he didn't care for it much and soon changed to hard cider, telling himself to be careful for he knew from experience that it could be dangerous. At the end of the dinner Jock Mackay rose to his feet and proposed a birthday toast to the Laird, and the Laird replied, and then it seemed that everyone wanted to get up and propose a toast to someone or something. Everyone was laughing and talking and the babble of sound spread from the great room out over the terrace and echoed above the quiet waters of the loch.

But it was the part after dinner that Smiler liked. The old piano was dragged from the Laird's study and Mrs. Mackay played and the piper piped and songs were sung and dances danced. Smiler, who soon picked things up, found himself part of reels, jigs and strathspeys that – with the help of his cider – set his head spinning. Laura helped him to pick up the movements and told him the names of the dances which Smiler found fascinating. They had *Strip the Willow*, the Strathspey dance, *Jenny's Bawbee* (which was done by Laura and Smiler and Mr. and Mrs. Mackay), and then a host of others: *Ye're Welcome Charlie Stuart*, *Roxburgh Castle*, *Dashing White Sergeant*, *Highlandman Kissed His Mother*, and *My Love She's But a Lassie Yet*.

Then two swords were taken down from their place on the wall above the wide fireplace and Laura did a sword dance. With her hair, tartan sash and skirts flying, Smiler thought she looked wonderful and he clapped his hands and shouted with the rest of the company in applause. After that each man and woman had to sing a song or tell a story or riddle. Smiler sitting with a glass of cider in his hand, face flushed from the dancing and singing, could see his turn coming. Quite suddenly it seemed that every story or song he had ever known had gone from his head and he dreaded the moment when his name would be called and all eyes would be on him.

When his turn came Laura called to him, "Song or story, Sammy?"

"A song, of course," said the Laird. "He's aye singing about the place like a bird."

From the piano Mrs. Mackay looked at Smiler and gave him a warm smile. Somehow her smile drove all the nervousness from him. He stood up and sang the first verse of the first song which came into his head and Mrs. Mackay soon picked up the melody on the piano.

Ye Mar'ners all, as you pass by,
Call in and drink if you are dry.
Come spend, my lads, your money brisk –
And pop your nose in a jug of this!

And here Smiler, remembering how his father used to do it and make him laugh, raised his cider glass and drank. Then he went through the whole song, and finished with the verse which his father always rounded off with a big wink and a swig at his glass.

Oh, when I'm in my grave and dead,
And all my sorrows are past and fled,
Transform me then into a fish,
And let me swim in a jug of this!

To his delight they made him sing the last verse again and they all joined in and raised their glasses on the final line.

After that the rest of the evening went by in a whirling and swirling of songs and games and buffoonery which set the great hall ringing. It was a great tidal wave of companionship and gaiety which finally swept Smiler away like flotsam on the flood and he found himself, exhausted but happy and his head reasonably clear, in his bedroom. The window was open and he rested his arms on the sill, looking out over the roofs and towers to the loch and the hills that framed it.

There was a movement behind him and Laura joined him, taking a place by his side at the window. They said nothing. They just leaned out, watching the night.

It was then that Smiler, not knowing what prompted him, began to tell Laura about himself.

He told her the whole story of the approved school and his escape and about all the adventures which had finally brought him to Scotland so that he could meet his father in October. He finished by saying, "The Laird knows – and now you do. But I don't want anyone else to know. You'll keep it secret, won't you, Laura?"

Laura touched his arm with her hand and said quietly, "Aye, I will, Sammy. But I'm glad you told me – and I'm sure your father will settle things fast when he gets back."

Then, as though for their special benefit, Nature put the final crown to a wonderful evening.

Slowly in the north, the dark sky began to lighten. From high in the heavens it was as though some unseen hand was slowly letting spill a great, pleated fold of silver, pink and grey silk. As the silk fell it spread wide at its base and was slowly lacquered with green, orange and pale purple washes of fire, all leaping upwards, flickering and shimmering about the swaying folds. Smiler watched spellbound. He'd never seen anything like it in his life before.

Beside him Laura said, "Yon's the Northern Lights."

As she spoke the tight gathering of fires at the apex of the curtain suddenly swiftly unfolded, flashing wide, and the whole sky was flooded with a blaze of silver and pink which swept round from the north encircling the entire heavens and then was gone.

* * *

All the visitors left on the Sunday evening. The following few days seemed very flat for Smiler. He polished up the silver and put it back in the safe, and he hid the key away in the staircase post. For the rest of the week the weather stayed hot and sultry except for two thunderstorms when the rain deluged down for about an hour. But the water from the storms did nothing to raise the level of the loch. Each day now it dropped a few more inches. By the end of the week Smiler had long recovered from feeling dull.

Between them, he and the Laird finished the extension to the wild-fowl pen. But they were both worried about the greylag gander. Laggy paddled on the bay or grazed in the meadow with the other wild fowl, but he showed no signs of wanting to fly. Once or twice as the Laird and Smiler watched him on the water, he would raise himself up and flap his wings, as though airing and exercising them – but he never made any move to take off.

They took him into the surgery and the Laird made an inspection of the wing in case it had not set properly.

When he had finished, he said, "It's as good as it ever was, Samuel M."

"Then why won't he use it?" asked Smiler.

The Laird considered this for a moment and then said, "Well, I can only suggest one thing. Say now you'd been a bonnie long jumper and you broke your leg. When it was mended – if you were of a certain turn of mind – you might not be too keen on risking it for the long jump again."

"You mean Laggy's scared to try to fly?"

"It could be, lad. He's got all the food and comfort he needs here without risking a flight. But I don't think we need worry. Every creature in nature needs more than food and safety. When the time comes and he sees the other greylags flying over, away to their breeding grounds. . . . Well, then, the mating instinct will be too strong for him. The need of a wife will hit him like a bolt from the blue and he'll be up and away. Aye, old Mother Nature won't stand any nonsense from him then."

So they put Laggy back with the other wild fowl and Smiler hoped that the Laird was right. But each evening when he took the boat out and Laggy followed him to the limit of the bay Smiler used to call to him, "Come on, you silly old Laggy – fly!"

However, Laggy's problem faded from Smiler's mind when that next weekend Laura arrived on the Saturday without the flag being flown for her. She brought up some supplies – but she had really come because a telegram had arrived at the farm for the Laird. It was from his married son in London to tell him that he was a grandfather. His son's wife had just given birth to a baby boy.

The Laird, who had been expecting the news, was very excited about this because it was his first grandchild. By now Smiler knew that the Laird had had two older sons but they had both been killed in the fighting long ago in Korea.

They all went into the great hall and they drank the health of the new baby and the Laird with a twinkle in his eye said, "Well, they've taken over long enough about it."

Laura, in her forthright way, said, "You ought to go down to London and see the baby, Laird."

"No, lass, I couldn't do that. There's too much here to do. Besides, I couldn't leave Samuel M., alone."

"Why not?" asked Smiler. "I could manage, and

I wouldn't mind. I'm not afraid of being here alone."

"And, anyway," said Laura, "I could come up and keep him company for a few days later on. Why don't you go?"

"I'll give it some thought," said the Laird.

"If you give it too much thought, you'll never go," said Laura bluntly. "You could do with a holiday away from here."

The Laird considered this, and then he rubbed his beard and gave Smiler a look over the top of his wire-rimmed spectacles. "You really think you could manage, lad?"

"Of course I could, sir."

"It's a big old place to be in alone."

"It doesn't scare me. And anyway, sir – if anything went wrong I could always fly the flag at half-mast."

"Aye, that you could."

"And I'd be up in a flash," said Laura. "So that's settled then. You can come back in the boat with me tomorrow morn and my father will drive you to Fort William for the London train."

"That's right," said Smiler.

The Laird smiled. "Ye've got it all fixed between you it seems. Still . . ."

"You're going," said Laura firmly.

"Of course you are, sir," said Smiler. "You haven't seen your son for ages. And now there's the baby."

The Laird slowly shrugged his shoulders. "Well, it seems I am. But only for a few days. It wouldn't be right to leave you here on your own any longer, though I must say you'll have enough work to do to keep you out of mischief and to send you dead to sleep the moment your head touches the pillow at night."

The next morning the Laird, looking quite different dressed in a tweed suit and with his beard carefully brushed and combed, went off in the boat with Laura and Smiler was left on his own. He stood on the jetty and waved to them as they went out of the bay. Then, when they were gone, he turned round and looked up at the castle. A pair of jackdaws sailed over the high turrets and a pack of hunting swifts screeched as they flashed above the terrace, hawking for flies and midges. Samuel M., Smiler thought, you're here all alone. You're the king of the castle! At this moment Bacon pushed his cold nose into his hand as though to remind him that he was not quite all alone.

Whistling to himself, Smiler walked off the jetty to begin his morning chores.

But Smiler would not have whistled so happily if he had known that at that moment he was being watched from the far southern shore of the loch. Hiding behind the boulder from which he had watched the castle before was Billy Morgan, field glasses to his eyes, and a can of beer on the ground at his side. He watched the boat with Laura and the Laird in it disappear into the heat haze down the loch and then came back to Smiler and followed him as he began to go about his morning work in the pens. Slowly he lowered the glasses, took a swig of his beer, and then rubbed his plump face thoughtfully. Being a man who had the habit of talking out loud to himself, he said, "Well now, Billy Morgan – what do you make of that, mate? The Laird away in his best suit with the girl, and that tow-headed lad left all on his own. Yes, Billy, what do you make of that after all your watchin' and plannin' and being eaten half to death by flies on this hillside? Has the moment come? Are you perched on the edge of riches? Are your Lucy Lockets at last going to ring with the sweet music of silver?" He took another swig of beer, and went on, "Who knows? Maybe yes, and maybe no. I think I'll have to take the long walk back and have a chat with that squint-eyed Willy McAufee." He stood up and smiled contentedly – but for all the plump wrinkles on his face his grey marble eyes remained cold.

*   *   *

Because he had extra work to do Smiler finished later that day. He had his supper in the kitchen and then he took the boat out with Bacon in it and Dobby swimming alongside. He fished outside the bay, but caught nothing. There was no wind and the loch was dead flat. After a while he let the boat drift down the cliffside of the island and leaned over and watched the big salmon move away from its lie as he passed. Dobby disappeared underwater just off his eating rock and stayed down for a very long time. By now Smiler was used to this and did not worry about the otter. When he reached the end of the island he unshipped the oars and rowed right round it, coming into the bay from the other side. As he pulled into the jetty Dobby surfaced some way out and came flopping up the jetty steps, his pelt dripping with water. Smiler watched as the otter gave himself a quick shake, ridding himself of water so that his coat was sleek and shining and dry again.

In the gloaming Smiler went back into the castle and lit his bedtime candle. Dark shadows in the hall and on the stairway danced away before his candle as he went up to the top landing. From the oil paintings the long line of Elphinstone ancestors looked down at him, their faces and eyes seeming to come alive in the wavering candlelight. Smiler found it all very eerie. Suppose the castle *was* haunted and the Laird, out of kindness, had never told him? A shiver ran down his spine. Then, because he was a sensible boy, he told himself not to be silly. But he was glad to have Bacon at his heels and pleased too when they came across Midas in one of the corridors. Midas, as though feeling lonely himself, rose ponderously to his feet and joined them.

Smiler slept that night with Bacon on the foot of his bed and Midas curled on the carpet near its head. He lay in bed with the window wide open. Now and again, before he dropped off to sleep, he saw the black flickering of a bat's silhouette waver across the pale night sky and caught the sound from the castle wood of the pair of long-eared owls that lived there calling to one another.

However, after a couple of days on his own, Smiler became quite used to his solitary state. On the third day Laura arrived early in the morning, just for an hour, to tell him that she would come again that weekend and stay some days with him. She couldn't come before because – they were into September now – the whole farm was busy harvesting and her mother couldn't spare her.

The following day was one of the hottest that Smiler could remember since he had been on the loch. The animals were listless and scarcely moved from the shade and showed little interest in their food, and Mrs. Brown gave only half the milk she usually did. Smiler himself felt that all the marrow had gone from his bones. He worked stripped to the waist and the sweat ran off him. His body now was as brown as a ripe hazel nut and his muscles were hard and firm.

He was too hot and tired to cook himself any supper. He had a glass of milk and some biscuits and then went out into the boat, hoping to find it cooler on the water. Bacon and Dobby went with him. Laggy, still showing no desire to fly, paddled as far as the bay mouth and then turned back. Stripped off to the bathing trunks which Laura had left for him, Smiler let the boat drift, too tired even to bother with fishing.

Close to the foot of the cliff, off Dobby's eating rock, Smiler threw the stone anchor overboard and let the boat swing on the length of the mooring rope. Bacon curled up on the stern seat and Dobby slid over the side to do some fishing.

Smiler sprawled himself belly down across the centre thwart, his head over the boat side and watched the antics of Dobby in the amber clear water below him. Although Dobby had lost a foot he was still a very strong swimmer. After a time Smiler lost sight of the otter and decided to take a swim himself. He stood on the thwart and dived into the water, the rocking of the boat behind him upsetting Bacon from the stern seat.

Smiler went down in a long, clean dive and then swam underwater towards the rock face. He held his breath for a long time, relishing the coolness of the water on his body. He came up close to Dobby's rock and hauled himself on to it. The top was covered with fish bones and tiny dried fish scales that glistened like pearls in the sunlight. After a time Dobby appeared, fishless, and climbed out on to the rock with Smiler. Finally Smiler lay back and went into a daydream, wondering where his father was at this moment. It would soon now be October. The *Kentucky Master* would be on her way home, steaming through the Atlantic. . . . And soon he, Smiler, would have to make his way to Greenock and get all the approved school mess cleared up. . . . And after that? Could he really ever become a vet? He'd learnt a lot from the Laird and had begun to read one of his books about veterinary surgery. But how could he do it? It all seemed a bit of a dream. October. Greenock. When he left here would he ever see the Laird again? Or Laura? Gosh, he hoped he would. Especially Laura.

At this moment Smiler heard Dobby stir. He sat up to see the otter sliding into the water. Feeling hot again Smiler dived into the water after the animal. As he went down, eyes open, close to the rock face of the cliff, he saw Dobby below and ahead of him. The otter swung back in a circle and flashed by him, the long, sleek form rolling and twisting, and headed for the underwater rock face. As Dobby neared the rock face and Smiler began to rise from want of breath, he saw a most extraordinary thing. Instead of Dobby turning away from the rock face and swimming along it, the otter suddenly seemed to go right through the rock and disappear.

Smiler came to the surface, puffing and blowing to get his breath. He frowned, puzzled at what he had seen. How could an otter swim through rock? He waited to see if Dobby would surface. But after a few minutes there was no sign of the otter.

After treading water for a while, Smiler porpoise-dived and swam down the submerged rock face as close as he could get. The water under the cliff was, although clear, in deep shadow. Smiler swam to the spot where Dobby had disappeared and reached out for the dark rock face. But his hands touched nothing. What he had thought was rock was dark shadow. His breath going, he let himself rise slowly to the surface, his hands outstretched into the shadow. As his head came out of water he felt his still submerged hands touch rock. Smiler held on to the rock and slowly his feet came up behind him. He quickly puzzled out the situation. In the face of the rock was a tall, narrow entry which was bridged at its top. The top, to which Smiler was clinging, was only about six inches underwater. With the loch at its normal level it would have been four or five feet under. Curious and intrigued, Smiler took a deep breath and dived down again. He went right to the bottom of the loch and found one side of the entrance. He began to work his way to the surface again holding on to the smooth side of the tall narrow archway.

Smiler went right to the top of the archway again. Holding it he popped his head out for fresh breath. He went down once more and traced up the other side of the entrance with his hands while his eyes tried to probe the darkness ahead of him. He was half-way up when something bright flickered far in the darkness. Suddenly, from out of the deep gloom, Dobby shot past Smiler, holding a finnoch in his jaws, the fish's white belly gleaming.

A few seconds later Smiler was sitting on the

eating rock where Dobby was crouched over his kill, chewing at the still body of the finnoch.

Smiler's face was very thoughtful. In his methodical, sensible way he began to figure things out.

Although he knew that otters could stay underwater for a long time, there was a limit. They just had to come up for breath. But sometimes Dobby would be under for ages. Although Smiler used to keep his eyes watchfully on the glass-smooth, calm water around the cliff he had never seen as much as half a whisker of Dobby's muzzle appear above the surface. Sometimes the animal was down so long that Smiler had given him up and rowed back to the castle. What he was thinking now was that the entrance could be to an underwater cave. The water level was only about six inches above the top of the archway. It couldn't be any higher inside the cave obviously. It might well be that, if he was brave enough to explore, he would find that above the level of the water in the cave there would be an air space. It could be quite a big space supplied with air from the cracks and crevices of the cliff in some way. And it was in there that Dobby sometimes went for fish and, when he had made a catch, he probably surfaced in the cave, climbed out, and had a leisurely meal. . . . While all the time, Samuel M., he told himself, you've been a-sittin' outside in the boat fussing about him.

Well, so it might be, thought Smiler. But one thing was for sure – he wasn't going to risk swimming underwater into a dark hole like that and end up getting stuck or running out of breath. Still, even as he decided he wasn't going to do it, his curiosity began to rise in him. The thing was a mystery and it was there right under his nose and it wasn't possible for him to ignore the challenge.

All the way back in the boat, and while he was getting ready for bed, Smiler kept thinking about the possibility of finding a secret underwater cave. Say there was a place inside where you could come to the surface and find all the air you wanted and rocks or a shelf to sit on? Just one clean dive in from the boat and, before half your breath was gone, up you would pop into another world. It was a pity that everything under the rock face was in such dark shadow. With a bit more light he might have risked it.

With a bit more light! He suddenly sat up in bed and smacked himself on the top of the head. You fool, Samuel M., he scolded himself. You fool! You could have all the light you wanted if you went at the right time! In the late evening the setting sun threw all the south side of the castle island cliffs in deep shadow – but at mid-day, when the sun was due south, it would be shining straight at the cliff, straight at the mouth of the underwater archway. He would be able to see a long way without even going through the archway if he didn't want to.

He lay back in bed knowing that when the sun was right the next day he would be around at the cliff face in the boat. Blimey! – a secret underwater cave! It might have stalactites hanging from the roof, if that was the word for the ones that hung and didn't rise from the floor. Or, less pleasant, there might be a skeleton in there of some old clansman from years and years ago, or of a boy like himself, caught exploring. . . . He pushed the thought from him. Anyway, even if it was only just a cave with nothing in it, it would be fun to show it to Laura.

137

He would scare her first by just diving clean off the boat and through the entrance without saying anything. . . . It took Smiler a long time to go to sleep that night.

The next morning as he worked around the castle he kept looking up at the sun and judging its position. Two or three times he went into the great hall to check the time on the big grandfather clock at the foot of the stairs.

All morning the sun seemed to dawdle up the cloudless sky like a heat-weary laggard, but eventually the clock showed ten minutes to twelve. Smiler ran down to the jetty where the rowing boat was moored and pulled out of the bay and round to the cliff face. He dropped the stone anchor some way up from the entrance and then, paying out the rope, let the boat drift down until he judged it was just level with the underwater archway.

Impatiently he jumped into the sunlit water under the cliff, took a deep breath, and porpoise-dived down, swimming strongly. In the blazing light of the sun the whole appearance of the place underwater had changed. Smiler could see the rough, narrow-arched entrance clearly. He swam down as deep as he could and grabbed the side of the entrance and looked through. The water was green and blue shot and adrift with little motes of light. He saw at once that the archway was only about two feet thick. Beyond it he could see an underwater strip of sandy loch floor sloping gently upwards.

Smiler went up, took another deep breath, and dived down again. This time he swam to the inner edge of the archway and looked up. Some way above him he could see the surface ripple of the water, making weird patterns from the light reflected from the sandy bottom – but he saw something else, too. Floating on the surface, proving to him that it was the surface and not some trick of light, was a short length of old tree branch that had got sucked through the archway somehow.

Although he had plenty of breath left to get back to the outer water and surface, Smiler gave himself a kick upwards towards the floating branch.

His head broke water and the first thing he was aware of was the echoing sound of water lapping against rocks where he had disturbed it.

Smiler looked around. He was in a large cave the sides of which rose up nearly twenty feet, converging to make a rough, dome-shaped roof. The wall of the cave on the righthand side of the entrance rose in a sheer, rugged sweep of rock. On the lefthand side the water washed gently over a smooth, flat layer of rock. The water was only about a foot deep. Beyond this, clear of the water, was a bank of small stones and broken rocks that sloped up to a small platform. The cave was lit by a shimmering, green light that came through the underwater entrance. But light came in, too, from another source. High up, almost in the domed roof and to one side of it, a thin, horizontal shaft of sunlight angled downwards to illuminate the small platform. Smiler guessed that this must come from some narrow slit in the rock face of the outside cliff.

Smiler swam to the bank of stones and boulders and climbed up on to the narrow platform of dry rock. The first things he saw were the dried-up bodies of two half eaten trout with a scattering of bones and fish scales around them. This was clearly

Dobby's eating place when he came fishing in the cave.

Standing on the platform, water dripping from him, Smiler took a good look around. On the far cave wall he could clearly see the high-water mark of the loch. He reckoned that when the loch was at its fullest, the water would be a foot deep over the platform on which he stood. At the back of the platform, where the cave wall ran up in craggy steps and ridges, was a stretch of loose soil and sand and a line of old drift wood and leaves which had been left there as the water receded. He looked up to the crack through which the roof light came. It was too far up for him to climb and explore. Then, as his eyes travelled down the rough face of the rock, he saw that about two feet above his head was a hole in the rock. For a moment Smiler almost ignored it, but then something about it brought his attention back to it sharply.

It did not look like a natural hole. It was about a foot high and a foot wide and its sides were sharply and regularly cut. Smiler realized that the hole had been chiselled and cut out of the rock face.

Finding footholds, Smiler hoisted himself up to the level of the hole and looked in. It was dark inside and he could see nothing. Smiler got his right arm free and groped inside the hole, feeling around with his hand. The hole ran back into the rock about two feet and Smiler's fingers touched nothing but the bare, dusty sides until his hand reached the end of the hole. There, instead of feeling the rough rock, his hand rested on something hard and dry which moved under his fingers. From the feel of it he knew that it was not a loose stone.

Panting with the effort of holding on to the rock face as he probed, Smiler got a grip on the object and pulled it towards him. Smiler got a firmer grip on the object, and then climbed down the few feet to the rock platform.

He sat down and rested the object between his legs. He stared at it, wondering what on earth it was. It was brown and roughly shaped like an outsized and pretty battered football. The whole thing was bound up tightly with a criss-crossing of thin leather thongs. The knots holding them had dried up so firmly that they defied Smiler's attempts to undo them.

Smiler sat there like an inquisitive ape which had been presented with something it had never seen before. He raised the object, which was fairly heavy, and shook it. There was the faintest rattle from within. He smelt it and it had a faint smell of old leather. The only thing which Smiler didn't do, which an ape might have, was to take a bite at it to see what it tasted like. He did, however, try to work one of the knots free with his teeth, but the knot-turns were set hard and unmovable.

Well, Samuel M., he thought, whatever is inside you're going to need a knife to get at it. For a horrible moment he wondered if there were a skull inside and what he could hear rattling were the loose teeth. The thought made him feel suddenly lonely and a bit scared in the cave. For all he knew any moment now, just because he was here and disturbing things, the roof might come crashing down – Holy Crikeys!

Almost before he knew he was doing it, Smiler was on his feet. He grabbed the brown football thing to his chest and took a fast header off the platform. He cleared the little shelf below, went deep down, and streaked through the underwater exit with panicky, froglike jerks of his legs.

Ten minutes later Smiler was back in the castle sitting at the kitchen table with the sharpest knife he could find. He sawed away at the binding thongs and realized now that they were thin strips of hide. And the brown, stiff wrapping, he guessed, was probably some kind of deer skin. Here and there on it were a few wet patches of browny-red hair. When all the thongs were cut, Smiler began to unwrap the stiff, hard, hide covering. Inside this was another covering of faded red cloth. This came away easily and out on to the table tumbled a heap of all shapes and sizes of small parcels, all wrapped in torn off pieces of stained and rotten linen sheet.

When Smiler unwrapped the first and biggest of these, he knew exactly what he had found in the cave. He just sat and stared at it wide-eyed and whispered to himself, "Holy Jumping Jumpers!"

Lying on the well-scrubbed table top was the great eight-pointed diamond star brooch of the Lady Elphinstone whose portrait hung at the top of the grand staircase. And, as Smiler unwrapped the other parcels, more and more of the Elphinstone treasure came to light. There was far more of it than just the jewels, rings and necklace that Lady Elphinstone was wearing in the painting. The kitchen table was a-glitter and a-sparkle with the fire of jewels, pearls, and gold and silver.

Smiler just sat and gawped at it all. Although he was overcome by the richness of the treasure, the thought that slowly obsessed his mind – and gave him a very odd sort of feeling – was that the last person who had looked at this fabulous sight was Sir Alec Elphinstone in 1745. He was the first one since then who had ever seen it! Holy Crikeys!

He suddenly leaped up and began to do a war-dance around the kitchen, waving and flailing his arms and shouting at the top of his voice. Midas growled from the doorway in protest and Bacon, who thought it was some new game, began to bark and cavort around the room with him. Only the cat on the windowseat who, like all cats, had long ago given up trying to humour or understand human beings, went quietly on with her grooming.

8

∽ The Skipper and the Chief Mate Come Aboard ∽

Smiler was so excited that it took him a long time to go to sleep that night – and when he did it was to dream wildly. He found himself marching with the old Sir Alec Elphinstone in the victorious army of Bonnie Prince Charlie, riding a shaggy pony and carrying a claymore miles too big for him. And then, when victory turned to defeat and rout, he was escaping with Sir Alec across the high hills, hiding in the corries and glens while the King's men searched for them. After days of hard tramping, they came back at last to the castle where Sir Alec, sad-faced, thanked him for his services and sent him away to his hill farm home. At home, his family all gathered round to hear his adventures – and it was a mixed up sort of family. Although his father was his father, his mother was somehow Mrs. Mackay and interested in nothing of his doings except to ask him had he always had enough to eat. She plied him now with mountains of food which Laura, red-faced from the hot range, brought to the table. . . .

He woke the next morning feeling exhausted and was horrified to find that he had gone to bed and left all the jewels on the kitchen table. He bundled them up in their original wrappings and put the whole lot in the safe. As the long, hot day dragged by he was itching to tell someone about his discovery. He wondered if Laura would come up for a quick visit later in the afternoon – which she did sometimes. After he had milked Mrs. Brown that afternoon he found a job to do up in the wood behind the castle so that he could watch the loch westwards for a sign of her boat. He had almost given up hope when he saw the boat coming, riding high on the silvery heat shine of the loch water. A few minutes later he heard the distant *put-put-put* of the motor.

He raced down to the jetty to meet her. When she stepped out of the boat carrying a large basket of fresh-baked bread and other provisions for him, he started to gabble away about his discovery and made no sense at all until Laura said firmly, "Stop rattling away like a loon, Sammy, or I'll think you've gone daft from loneliness up here. Now begin at the beginning."

So Smiler calmed himself down and began at the beginning and Laura listened wide-eyed and, when Smiler had finished she said, sounding very like her mother, "You're no pulling my leg, are you?"

"Of course I'm not!" shouted Smiler. "Come on, I'll show you!" He grabbed her arm and began to pull her up to the castle so impetuously that her basket overturned. There was more delay while the bread and provisions were gathered up, except for one scone which Bacon grabbed and disappeared with.

In the castle, Smiler opened the safe. In a few moments all the jewels and treasure were laid out in front of Laura. Smiler watched her grow more wide-eyed at the sight of the sparkling, gleaming hoard, and he shifted impatiently from one foot to the other.

Laura slowly looked up at him and said, "Sammy . . . you're the boy wonder! The Laird will never know how to thank ye." Her eyes went back to the jewels. "Aye, look at the bonnie beauties."

Then to Smiler's surprise she picked up the eight-pointed star on its head band and slipped it on to her forehead. Grinning at Smiler, she asked, "How do I look?"

"Smashing," said Smiler. And she did, with her dark hair flowing to her shoulders and the diamonds of the great star blazing on her warm, brown forehead.

Taking the star off, she said, "Aye – yon Sir Alec of those days must have been a canny man. He knew the Prince's cause was lost forever. Like a good Scot he hid the lot away and said nothing to anyone. Not even to his good lady because he knew the Butcher's men had ways of making folk talk. He meant always to come back but it was not to be. He died within weeks, they say, of a fever, without a chance to say where the jewels were."

"And no one knew about the cave," said Smiler. "I reckon he found it as a boy when he was swimming and he said nothing. Just in case it came in handy sometime. And I'd never have found it if it hadn't been for old Dobby. Gosh! Just think – the Laird will be able to do all he wants now." He grinned. "You might get your farm."

Laura looked up at him and a slow smile spread across her face and she said, "Then all I'll need is a handsome and hard-working husband to go with it. Can you think of anyone of our acquaintance, Sammy, who would meet the bill?"

Suddenly Smiler found himself blushing. Quickly he leaned over the table and began to collect the jewels. "I'd better get these back in the safe," he said.

*   *   *

146

An hour later Laura left the castle. Hers had only been a flying visit to see that Smiler was all right and to bring his provisions. She explained that she would not be up again for three or four days because things were so busy on the farm at the moment. The Laird would certainly have returned from London by then and she would bring him back.

When darkness began to fall Smiler went into the kitchen and made himself some supper. He put it all on a tray and carried it up to the main hall where he ate it. After supper he read more of the book on veterinary surgery which the Laird had lent to him. It was pretty hard going and there were lots of words that Smiler did not know. He went into the study and brought back the Laird's dictionary. He kept at it for over an hour. But his mind was not really on his task. He kept thinking about the Elphinstone treasure and how pleased the Laird would be about its recovery and how he would now be able to do all the things he wanted to do. Finally he put the book down and he curled up comfortably in the Laird's big velvet, wing-backed chair and had a good think about himself and his father and what they would do once all this approved school business had been cleared up. Maybe he could get his father to find a shore job. After all he was a good cook and there were plenty of places he could get work. But he was doubtful about it. His father had this thing about the sea. Smiler realized that if you had a thing about a thing and it was kind of in your blood . . . well, there wasn't much you could do about it. It was like himself now . . . he knew he never wanted to live anywhere but in the country and to work always at something to do with animals. His education hadn't been up to much so far, but he was still young enough to do something about that. If he kept at it . . . well, the old book on veterinary surgery would one day become child's play to him. "Yes, Samuel M.," he said aloud, "you've got to get your head down and work. That's what you've always got to do if you want something what's really worth having."

He lay back in the chair and day-dreamed about being a vet. Maybe, too, he could have a farm to sort of go with the business. Then he remembered how Laura had sat at the great table, not so long ago, wearing the eight-pointed Elphinstone star. She'd looked smashing. . . . For sure the Laird would buy her a farm, and then all she would need – he recalled her words now without any embarrassment because there were only Bacon and Midas to see him – would be a handsome and hard-working husband to go with it. His eyes flickering with sleepiness, he grinned and said aloud, "Well that does for you, Samuel M. Hard work you could manage, but nobody would call you handsome. . . ." And with that thought he drifted off to sleep.

Long, long after midnight Smiler woke with a start to hear Bacon barking. Even in half sleep Smiler knew that it was Bacon's half-puzzled, half-enquiring bark. Bacon seldom used an angry bark. He was much too trusting a sort of dog.

Smiler opened his eyes and was immediately dazzled. The light of a strong torch was full on his face. Beyond its fierce glow he could see nothing. Startled, he started to move from the chair, but a hand moved out and pushed him firmly back.

A man's voice said, "Just you sit nice an' easy

there, matey. We'll have some proper light going in a couple of ticks."

Still trying to puzzle things out, sleep not fully gone from him, Smiler stayed where he was. It was a calm, not unfriendly voice and had a Cockney accent.

"That's the ticket," said the man.

Farther down the great hall Smiler saw the beam of another torch break out and he watched as the person holding it moved around. Within a short while the person with the other torch had found the bedroom candles at the foot of the stairs and also the big oil lamp which stood on a small side table. The candles and lamp were lit and, as the great hallway was filled with their soft light, the torches were switched off.

Although he did not know his name, Smiler found himself looking up at the plump face of Billy Morgan. Billy Morgan was dressed in a green windbreaker, navy blue jersey and shabby old corduroy trousers. He gave Smiler a nod and a smile, but it was the kind of smile which never touched his eyes. Instinctively Smiler felt there was something wrong with the smile.

Smiler said, "Who are you . . . and what do you want here?"

Billy Morgan nodded approvingly. "Two sensible questions in the circs, lad. But, sorry to say – you ain't goin' to get an answer to the first one. Just sit tight and be a good lad, and nobody'll lay a finger on you. Just think of me as the Skipper and 'im down there –" he nodded to where the other man was putting the oil lamp on the far end of the table, "– as the Chief Mate. Though if either **of us**, matey, was daft enough to ship to sea to find a fortune then we'd need our Uncle Teds examined. The best pickings is on shore and for pickings we have come."

Smiler digested this and, because he was no fool, though he was pretty scared by now, he wasn't long in putting two and two together.

The man at the other end of the table was very small and thin and his shoulders were hunched up around his neck giving him a jockeyish look. He wore a flat cap, a muffler round his neck, a shabby jacket much too small for him, and a pair of flannel trousers so big that they flapped around his ankles as he moved. He had a narrow, pointed face, creased with wrinkles, and seemed pretty old to Smiler. As he moved about he kept up a thin, tuneless whistling to himself.

Screwing courage into himself Smiler said firmly, "You two better get out of here before I set the dogs on you. They'll . . . they'll tear you to pieces."

Billy Morgan gave his humourless laugh and said, "Good try, lad. Good try. But not good enough. Still – seven out of ten for guts. No, no . . . we been watchin' this little tickle for weeks waiting for the right moment and there ain't a thing we don't know, me and the Chief Mate. Them tikes of yours is just too friendly. 'Cepting Midas, of course. And 'im you got to step on before he turns nasty. Now, you just sit there nice and easy while we does our business." He called to the other man, "All right, Chiefy. No trouble this end. Get the key – and let's make it Uncle Dick."

The Chief Mate, whistling to himself, pulled a sheet of paper from his pocket, consulted it, and then moved to the side of the fireplace and began to fiddle with one of the carvings of the wainscoting. After a moment Smiler saw a small panel spring back. The man groped inside and then shook his head.

"Number One empty, Skipper," he reported.

"Get on with it, then. It's got to be in one of 'em according to reliable information received."

Glued to his chair, his eyes watching every movement, Smiler knew exactly what they were about. There were a lot of secret hiding places in the hall. The Laird had shown some of them to him from time to time. His own fear suddenly left him, driven right out of his mind as he realized fully what was happening – and just what it could mean to the Laird. These men were thieves and they were after the Laird's silver and – Holy Crikeys! There was more than just the silver in the safe now!

Before he could help himself Smiler got up from the chair and shouted, "Just you two listen to me! There ain't nothing –"

Billy Morgan's big right hand shot out and pushed him roughly back into the chair.

"Easy, lad. There ain't a ting-a-ling you can do. So sit tight and keep yourself in one piece. Just think of it in a sensible way. The Laird's got plenty and he ain't goin' to miss a few bits of old silver. And what's it to you, anyway? You're just a workin' lad like ourselves, and workin' lads must eat. Nothin' you can do, anyways. Two to one. Nobody's going to say you could have done anything."

From down the hall where the Chief Mate had been fiddling with another hiding place under one of the windows, the whistling stopped, and he announced, "Number Two empty."

"Not to worry," said Billy Morgan easily. "Four more to go yet. Got to be in one of 'em. He moves it around, he does, the Laird. Cagey old cove. Likeable, though. Pity to do his silver, but there it is. There ain't no end to the class war."

He winked at Smiler, but Smiler only glowered back at him. For all his easy talk he could tell now that this man was a real villain. His eyes never smiled and he seemed very sure of himself. But Smiler was more concerned now with the Chief Mate. He had a list of hiding places around the hall and if the one in the stairway post was on the list Smiler knew that there was nothing he could do to save the silver – and the Elphinstone treasure which was in the safe with it. Anxiously he kept his eyes on the Chief Mate. But, as he watched him, his mind was busy on another problem. The man in front of him knew Midas' name, and they had this list, and they'd been watching the castle for a long time – but no amount of watching could have given them the hiding places. Somebody else must have done that. Smiler had an idea who that might have been. It wasn't a good thing to think about someone he had never met, but from what Laura had said about Willy McAufee. . . . Well, he didn't have a very good reputation, and it could have been him. Unseen by the Skipper, he crossed his fingers and hoped that the Laird had never shown Willy the present hiding place of the key.

Within ten minutes the Chief Mate had exhausted all the hiding places on his list. There was no sign of the key and he broke off his whistling to announce, "That's the lot, Skipper. No key." He sat on the end of the long table, floppy trouser legs swinging and began to whistle to himself.

Billy Morgan screwed his face up in thought and began to pull at his chin with the fingers of one hand. Staring up into the shadowed recesses of the hall ceiling, he said to no one in particular, "No key. No silver. Well, well. . . . It's enough to make a man of poor spirit weep. But not you, Skipper, 'cos you knows there's silver here, and you knows it's in the safe, and all safes must have keys. And that Laird, being a canny Scot, is a hard-thinking, far-seeing man. Now then . . ."

He took a turn or two up and down in front of the fireplace in silence for a while. Smiler watched him while the Chief Mate swung his legs and whistled faintly and tunelessly.

After a moment or two Billy Morgan came back and stood in front of Smiler. Then, quite surprisingly, he said to Smiler, "And what would you do in my position, lad? Take the bad fall of the cards and pull out of the game to eat disappointment pie? Or, like a real sport, put on your best smile and ask Lady Luck for just another dance? Don't bother to answer, lad. We've got a real sticky tarbaby of a question. We must give it the best of our thought which can't be done on a dry gullet."

He went to the terrace door and came back with a large shabby rucksack from which he pulled a can of beer. He sat himself on a chair by the fire where he could watch Smiler and opened the can. He drank his beer, his eyes seldom leaving Smiler. His face wrinkled and creased itself with his passing thoughts so that he vaguely reminded Smiler of a fat rabbit munching on its food, the little wings of fair hair on either side of his head sticking up like small ears.

After a few minutes, during which he finished his

beer, his face suddenly moved into a smile and he nodded his head approvingly, "Aye – that's the ticket. Never say die – even though you can hear the hearse at the door. On your plates of meat, lad."

Smiler said, "What do you mean?"

"I means stand up, lad. On your feet. We're going to deal with this problem real methodical and not to say logical or my name's not . . . well, whatever it is. Stand up!" The command was curt and sharp.

Smiler slowly stood up.

"Chiefy," said Billy Morgan, "go through his Lucy Lockets."

The Chief Mate, without interrupting his whistling, came up the room and began to run his hands through Smiler's pockets, emptying all the contents on to the nearby table. Smiler made no protest. At the moment there was nothing he could do or say. They hadn't got the key and that was all that he cared about.

Billy Morgan went to the table and sorted through the small pile of belongings. None of it interested him, except a stout brown envelope in which Smiler kept the wages that the Laird had paid him weekly. Billy Morgan half-pulled the folded pile of notes from the envelope, riffled their edges with his thumb and said, "Not bad, not bad. A nice little pot of honey. Well, we'd better have it in case it's all we get." He put the envelope into his own pocket.

Unable to stop himself Smiler shouted, "You're a rotten old thief!"

Billy Morgan shrugged his shoulders and with a humourless smile said, "A tea-leaf, yes, lad. But not all that old. And far from rotten. Sound as a bell, in fact. But there's no need to apologize. I take no offence."

The Chief Mate stopped his whistling and said, "If that's all we're going to get, let's go, Skipper. There ain't goin' to be any more because there ain't no key. The Laird must have found a new hiding place since –"

Billy Morgan silenced him with a wave of his hand and said, "Don't give up, Chiefy. The boat's sound, the breeze is nothing and yours truly's at the helm. There's no key on the boy, that's true. And that's what I wanted to know first. Step by step you climb to success. It could 'ave been on him. But it isn't. That's step one cleared. Now for step two." He smiled at Smiler and asked, "You savvy what that is, lad?"

"If I did, I wouldn't tell you," said Smiler firmly.

"Ah, beginning to get a bit saucy, are we? Very nice. Like to see a boy of spirit. Give me a lad with backbone any time." He reached out and patted Smiler's shoulder, and then said suddenly, "You've seen the silver, ain't you?" When Smiler did not reply, he said affably, "Oh, yes, you 'ave. You was 'ere for the Laird's party. The 'ero of the hour with your salmon and all – that you won't deny."

"I'm not telling you anything," said Smiler.

Unruffled, Billy Morgan said, "Then let me tell you something. You've seen the silver 'cos you had the job of cleaning it. And the odds is that you know where the key is because the Laird, bless his tartan socks, is a nice old trusting cove when he likes someone. And like you he does is the way the chorus of the song goes around these parts. So to save yourself and us a lot of hubble-bubble why don't you just tell us where it is?"

Suddenly angry, Smiler shouted, "Why don't you just push off?"

To Smiler's surprise the man beamed at him, and then said, "Very interesting. Oh, very – for them, like me, what can read between the lines." He turned to the Chief Mate and said, "Take a lesson, Chiefy, in how to be a success. In other words, you got to use your loaf if you wants to eat cake. Now, when I asks our friend 'ere to tell us where the key is – what does he say? He tells us to push off. *Not*, you will notice, that he don't know where the key is, or that wild 'osses wouldn't make him tell us anything. No, Chiefy, he just says to push off. A rudeness I over-looks because it tells me what I want to know. He knows where the key is. Don't you, lad?"

Smiler, lips pressed tight together, his face glowering with obstinacy, said nothing.

"Very good," said Billy Morgan. "Oh, very good."

Suddenly he thrust out his right hand and pushed Smiler roughly backwards so that he collapsed into the winged armchair.

"That," said the man, "is only a tiny taste to show you I can be rough and very ready if the circs demand it. But for now, just sit there and think things over, lad. I'm going to do the same with another beer. Stubborn I can see you are, and no fool, and it is ditto and doubled for your humble 'ere. Very well then, we'll both do a little thinking. There's always some way to loosen up a stiff tongue."

Billy Morgan went back to his chair and settled himself with another can of beer. The Chief Mate, following a nod from Billy Morgan, went and sat near the terrace doorway, a thin trickle of whistling coming from his pursed lips as he watched Smiler.

Smiler sat in his chair and also did some thinking. In a curious way, he was not frightened now. He was, in fact, very angry with himself. Samuel M., he thought, you didn't use your head. This Skipper man isn't any fool. You should never have let go and told him to push off.

He sat there, wondering and puzzling away at what he could do . . . or more importantly, what they would do. It was no good trying to make a dash to get down to the boat and row away. The Chief Mate's eyes were always on him and so were the Skipper's. The moment he made a move they would both be after him. Looking towards the terrace, too, he realized that he must have slept for a long time in his chair before the men had arrived. The sky was beginning to lighten very faintly with the coming of dawn. He screwed himself round in his chair and looked at the grandfather clock at the foot of the stairs. Its hands showed half past four.

Seeing his action, Billy Morgan smiled, nodded, and said, "Don't worry about the old tempus, lad. We got all the bird-lime in the world to think up something really tongue-loosening for you. And if we don't – well we can always beat the truth out of you. Not that I go for violence, mind you. Not, that is, unless the circs don't give me no option."

Smiler said, "You're wasting your time. Even if you beat me I couldn't tell you where the key is 'cos I don't know."

Billy Morgan shook his head. "Too late, me old cock sparrer. Oh, much too late to be anything like the genuine article."

Billy Morgan sat there, thinking, quite undisturbed by the thin whistling of the Chief Mate. Midas lay snoring at the fireside and Bacon was stretched out asleep under the table. Smiler huddled back in his chair, a dark scowl of thought and self-displeasure over his tanned and freckled face. Outside the sky grew paler and a brisk morning wind came sweeping down the loch from the east, raising a choppy ripple on the waters, and from the island shores the sandpipers and redshanks began to call. Distantly Smiler heard Mrs. Brown give a low moo to greet the coming morning. Nearer, on the roofs above the terrace, came the cooing of the fantails and other pigeons. A few moments later one of the fantails came hovering low over the terrace and then sailed through the open doors and perched on the back of Smiler's chair.

Billy Morgan eyed the bird and said, "The dove of peace, eh, matey? Or it could be, if you was to be sensible. A real little paradise is all this place. Bird and beast and man all trustin' one another. Just like it should be. And real grateful, too, I am to that old bird because it gives me a notion for openin' up that safe without trouble."

He stood up and approached Smiler.

"Stand up, lad. Smartish now." His face creased with its cold smile, and the red tip of his tongue ran around the edges of his lips.

Smiler stood up. Billy Morgan produced a long length of cord from his windbreaker pocket and said, "Turn round. Hands behind."

For a second or two Smiler contemplated making a dash for freedom but decided against it. He would get nowhere. He turned round and Billy Morgan lashed his hands firmly together, leaving a long length of cord trailing from them to act as a lead.

Billy Morgan said, "Right. Come along with me." He gave Smiler a push towards the terrace door and followed at his side, holding the length of cord. At the door he said to the Chief Mate, "Get down to the boat and bring me the troubled-Harold."

Then, with a jerk on Smiler's cord, he led the way along the terrace and down the steps at the far end to the garden and headed for the meadow and the water-fowl pens.

The Chief Mate disappeared in the direction of the jetty.

Smiler, puzzled now to know what the Skipper had in mind, and not having any idea what a troubled-Harold was, went obediently across the meadow to the wild-fowl pens and the strip of beach where he had landed his salmon. Twenty yards out Laggy and a motley collection of water fowl were swimming around feeding and making their morning toilet, flapping their wings and bobbing their heads and necks underwater. Far up the loch the faces of the hills were dark with shadows, but the sky above them was now a pale wash of faded colours as the dawn began to strengthen.

They halted at the water's edge. Billy Morgan stared around him, his eyes sweeping over the water-fowl pens and the ripple-streaked island bay.

"Nice," he said to himself. "Oh, very nice. A great and good work the Laird is a-doin'. The Laird and you, lad, real angels of mercy to any bird or beast in trouble. Jam-tarts full of love for 'em. Wouldn't 'arm a hair of a hide or a wing of a feather. Lovely to see. Highly recommendable. And you're a clever man, too, Skipper. Real clever. There's always a way if you use your loaf." He looked round to see the Chief Mate approaching. "Ah, here comes Chiefy with troubled-Harold."

Smiler turned and saw the Chief Mate coming

along the beach. A cold shock of apprehension swept through him as the mystery of troubled-Harold was solved. The Chief Mate was carrying a double-barrelled shotgun.

Smiler turned to Billy Morgan and said, "What do you want that for? Look here –"

"Easy, lad," said Billy Morgan. "Easy. No need to lose your wool."

He took the gun from the Chief Mate and handed the lead rope to him to hold.

Billy Morgan took a couple of cartridges from his pocket and loaded the gun. Then he cocked an eye at Smiler and said, "You gettin' the idea, lad? No? Then I'll tell you. You knows where the key is – but you won't tell me. So, how do I find the right tongue-loosening oil for a stubborn lad? Easy. Always a way to do a deal with the most awkward of customers – if you knows their soft spot. And your soft spot is animals. Take old Laggy out there. Everyone round 'ere knows about Laggy and what you and the Laird 'ave done for him. Take all the other animals – and take 'em I will, one by one with this –" he smacked the stock of the shotgun smartly with the flat of his hand and went on, his voice cold and menacing "– unless you finds your tongue!"

"You wouldn't dare! You rotten devil, you wouldn't dare!" Smiler shouted.

"Oh, yes, I would, lad," snarled Billy Morgan. "I'd take Laggy and Dobby and Midas and your precious Bacon . . . the whole boiling lot one by one unless you talks. You don't believe me? Here, watch this for a beginning!"

He swung round, raised the shotgun, and took aim at Laggy swimming a few yards away on the water.

Seeing the movement, Smiler gave a wild cry and flung himself at the man, kicking out at him as he fired. But Smiler never reached the Skipper for the Chief Mate, with surprising strength for such a small man, held the cord firmly and jerked him to a halt so roughly that Smiler spun round and nearly fell over.

The sound of the shot thundered in Smiler's ears and he saw the spread pattern of the shotgun pellets raise a white trail of foam on the water. As he saw the spouting water, he realized that his shout and lunge forward had put the Skipper off his aim. The shot had fallen just short of Laggy and the ducks. Then he saw something else, something that, for a moment, made him forget the savageness of the Skipper. The ducks, mallards, pintails, pochards, and shovellers went up in an explosion of flight, all taking off in a flurry of wings and webbed feet beating at the water. But the thing that held Smiler transfixed was that as they went, Laggy went with them. The greylag was so shocked and frightened that he forgot his fear of his well-mended wing. With a loud *gang-gang-gang* of alarm his great wings opened and his big feet thudded on the water, thrusting him forward. Neck outstretched, wing tips hammering at the ripples, he went forward in wild alarm and in a few seconds was air-borne.

Forgetting the two men, Smiler saw Laggy rise, swing up in a great curve, and then, high above the low flying duck, turn and head westwards down the loch, wings beating strongly. Within a few moments the high-flying gander was hidden from sight by the tall towers of the castle.

Although Smiler was shaking all over with shock, there was a small part of him that sang with gladness for the greylag. Laggy was up and away and free, really free to join his own kind.

A hand fell on his shoulder and Billy Morgan spun him round. "Well, lad. That's just a taste. If you hadn't put me off, that there bird would 'ave been a goner. So what do you say?"

Recovering now, his face a stony, stubborn mask, Smiler looked at the Skipper. He would have liked to kill him. He was a dirty, rotten so-and-so. Even now, he had to hold himself in to stop his impulse to jump forward and kick and pummel the brute. But, for all his anger and contempt for the man, an icy cold part of Smiler's brain was sending clear and sensible signals. If he didn't tell where the key was then this man would carry out his threat. If the Laird were in his place now, he knew exactly what the Laird would do. The Laird, as he did, loved all living things. If Laggy *had been* killed, then not all the silver and precious stones in the world could have brought him back. Or Dobby, Midas, Bacon and Mrs. Brown and all the others.

Smiler said, "I'll get you the key."

"Aaaah!" Billy Morgan sighed with pleasure. "Now that makes sense. Good sense." Turning to the Chief Mate he said, "Untie him, Chiefy. He's learnt his lesson. We'll have no more hubble-bubble from 'im."

Smiler said nothing. He was beginning to understand the man's way of speaking, and he was thinking to himself that from now on he was really going to use his loaf – and if he could cause trouble he would.

As he turned away to walk back to the castle between the two men, the sun suddenly lipped the high crests of the hills and he felt Bacon press his cold muzzle into his hand.

9

∽ The Distress Signal ∽

With the coming of the sun the weather changed. The wind which for weeks had been light and from the east swung a hundred and eighty degrees through the north to the west. Big thunder-heads of cloud began to pile up over the seaward end of the loch. With its change the wind strengthened and the ripples on the water grew rapidly to long, deep wave troughs, scud and foam breaking from their crests. Within an hour the sun was hidden by a pall of dark grey clouds and fierce rain squalls raced up the loch from the west in hissing, grey veils.

Sitting at the big table in the hall watching the two men, Smiler could hear the skirl of leaves eddying along the terrace and the constant sough and sigh of the wind through the pines at the back of the castle. The changed weather matched his mood, dark and gloomy. Although he couldn't see what else he could have done, he kept blaming himself for what had happened. After all, he was in charge of the place and he had failed in his duties. If he had really used his wits he might have made the Skipper think that he had no idea where the key was. And now – he looked down the table. At the far end was the Laird's silver and the collection of stained linen packets that held the Elphinstone jewels.

When he had produced the key and the two men had emptied the safe they had soon found the jewels. Even the Chief Mate's wrinkled face had lightened with joy at the sight and his whistling had grown louder. The Skipper had been so elated that a shade of warmth had come into his eyes. He had said, gloating over the jewellery, "Look at it, Chiefy. The biggest haul of tom-foolery you could wish for!"

When he had asked Smiler where the jewels had come from, Smiler had really used his loaf. He had told the Skipper that the Laird, just before he had left for London, had found a secret cupboard in one of the tower rooms – for which he had been searching for years – and the jewels had been there. Smiler had done this deliberately because he was already planning to cause trouble.

The Chief Mate was now on guard at the terrace door, holding the shotgun. The Skipper was at the end of the table, methodically beginning to pack the silver and jewels into his big rucksack, making ready to leave. Coming back to the castle from the beach Smiler had seen down by the jetty the boat in which they had arrived. It was a sturdy craft with an outboard motor. Even with the bad weather which was now racing in from the sea, Smiler knew that they would have no trouble in getting away. He knew, too, that it would be hopeless to try and follow them in the Laird's small rowing boat. It would be swamped the moment he got outside the bay.

His mind teasing away at all sorts of schemes for outwitting the men, Smiler watched the Skipper packing the rucksack. Samuel M., he thought, you've got to find a way. There's got to be a way. Just think.

His freckled face was stubborn and set with thought. There just had to be a way. But how? Even if, when the rucksack was packed, say, he made a grab for it and ran . . . how could he ever get past the Chief Mate at the door? And if he *could* dodge the Chief Mate and make for their boat they would be peppering him with gunshot before he got it started. He needed time . . . time to get safely away. How on earth could he get safely past the Chief Mate? Come on, Samuel M., he scolded himself, think. There's got to be some way. He looked at the Chief Mate. Small and ancient looking he might be but he could be a fast mover and thinker. He had shown that when he had jerked Smiler back fiercely to keep him off the Skipper. Smiler's eyes moved away from him to look at the Skipper. As he did so, he saw the stairway post that had held the key and then. . . ! It suddenly came to him! What a fool!

Without any movement of expression to show his sudden excitement, he let his eyes travel up the stairs. Well, of course, you fool, he told himself. If you can't go out the front and you can't risk the back way through the kitchen – then you have to go some other way. These men might know a lot about the castle from, probably, Willy McAufee – but they couldn't know everything. And he, Smiler, knew his way around the castle now as well as the Laird.

Still keeping a stubborn, dejected look on his face, Smiler began to work it out. Once he had his hands on the rucksack, all he had to do was to sprint up the stairs and lose himself in the maze of corridors and tower steps. At the back of the castle there was one tower with a stairway which ran down to a little door that led out on to the battlement wall at the back. Because of the rising slope of the hill it was only a ten or twelve foot jump to the ground.

Excitement began to bubble inside Smiler. That's

it, Samuel M. That's it. Once free of the castle he knew exactly what to do. . . .

From the end of the table as he packed away the last of the Elphinstone treasure and silver, Billy Morgan squinted up at him and said, "Well, lad, that's the lot. And as sweet and unexpected a tickle as a man could wish for." He looked out at the terrace and the distant view of the loch. "Dirty weather blowin' up. In another half-hour only a good boat could live out there. But for your own good, seein' as you've been so helpful and I wish you no harm, we'll take the oars from your boat so you can't try anything stupid like followin' us. Right then, let's be goin' with our load of honey."

He picked up the rucksack by its straps and walked up the room. Smiler sat where he was. Billy Morgan shook his head sadly. "You come with us as far as the jetty, lad. Not trusting you out of my sight till there's water between us. On your plates of meat and move."

Smiler rose from his chair and went to the head of the table which was only a couple of yards from the great stairway. As the man came up to him he knew that this was the only moment he was going to have. Once outside he wouldn't get two feet away without the gun peppering him around the legs.

He took a deep breath and told himself, "This is the moment, Samuel M. Work fast and keep your head."

Swinging the rucksack in his hand, Billy Morgan came up the length of the table. Outside the wind whistled with a sudden squall and a quick splattering of rain swept across the terrace. Smiler turned, as though to walk ahead of the man, but he hardly had his back to him when he swung back swiftly and punched at Billy Morgan's plump stomach with the full force of his right fist. The result was gratifying. Smiler's muscles over the past months had grown hard and strong. The breath wheezed out of Billy Morgan and he doubled up, instinctively clutching at his injured midriff with both hands so that the rucksack fell to the polished boards.

Smiler was on the rucksack like a flash and leaping up the great stairway three steps at a time. He didn't look back to see what was happening, but he heard the Skipper shout and then the sound of feet thudding across the floor.

Holding firmly to the precious rucksack Smiler shot up the stairs. He swung round the landing post at the top, raced by the portraits of the elegant Lady Elphinstone and the warlike Sir Alec, and disappeared into a corridor like a hunted rabbit going into a warren. Behind him he heard an angry bellow from the Skipper. The whole plan of the castle clear in his mind, Smiler sprinted down the corridor, swung left, charged up a flight of stairs and began to work his way by a devious route towards the tower which would give him escape to the woods at the back of the castle. Behind him he could hear the noise of the following men. But as he reached the top of the stairs, he was aware of something which he knew could be more than awkward for him. He had forgotten Bacon who had been resting under the great hall table. And here now, hard on his heels, was Bacon, barking his head off and prancing ahead of him as though this was some splendid new game. He knew that, as long as Bacon was with him, the dog's barking would give the men a lead to his whereabouts.

He ran down another corridor. Then, thinking fast, he stopped by a bedroom door and opened it. He swung half in and Bacon, thoroughly enjoying the lark, dashed into the room past him. Smiler turned on his heels and jumped into the corridor, slamming the door. As he raced away he could hear Bacon barking in a frenzy behind the door.

For two or three minutes Smiler ran through the top corridors and pelted up and down stairs until the sounds of pursuit faded behind him. Satisfied that he had a good lead, he headed for the back tower.

He came darting out on to the low battlement top, hoisted himself up on to the parapet and jumped. He landed with a crash right in the heart of a large rhododendron bush and rolled in a tangle of leaves and branches to the ground. The next second he was on his feet and heading at top speed for the pine trees. When he was well in the pines he stopped and looked back, listening, his shoulders rising and falling as he fought for breath. There was no one in sight behind, but he could hear, very faintly, the sound of Bacon's barking. To make it easier for running he slipped the rucksack over his shoulders and raced away along a small path that led to the southern cliffside of the island. As he did so, he was not relishing the moment to come.

In a short while he was out of the trees on to the close turf of the cliffs. The wind coming up the loch, full of rasping rain squalls, smacked hard into his face. The whole loch as far as he could see was a wilderness of white-capped, rolling waves.

Smiler, head lowered against the wind, ran across the turf to a point on the cliffs immediately above the underwater entrance to the cave. He halted on the edge and shuddered. There was a rough jumble of loose boulders for about ten feet below him and then a sheer drop – into water that was beating against the base of the cliff in great, swinging rollers, leaden and sullen looking with spouting spume and froth marbling them.

Smiler looked back to the trees. There was no one in sight. Then he looked down at the water and his heart sank. Holy Crikeys, it was going to be like jumping off the top of a church tower! For a moment he thought it was too much, that he couldn't do it. . . . Then self-anger burst inside him and he shouted aloud into the wind, "You got to do it, Samuel M. You got to do it!"

The next minute he was scrambling down amongst the loose rocks and boulders to the point where he could make his jump. He looked down and saw Dobby's rock, the waves now crashing over the top of it. But it was only a brief look because he knew that the longer he looked the more likely he was not to jump.

As the rain and wind battered at his face, he took a deep breath, grabbed his nose tight with his right hand – and jumped.

It was the most extraordinary three or four seconds of Smiler's life. As he leaped out into space, the fierce wind took him and, from the resistance offered by the hump of the rucksack on his back, it swung him round in a slow spin like a lazy top. He went down to the water, feet first. One moment he was looking at rock face and the next at the loch. Trees, cliffs, loch, hills and scudding clouds and rain storms swept before his eyes in a slow whirl – and then he hit the water with an almighty bang. A great spout of foam shot skywards and then peeled off into a ragged, dying ring of wind-torn spray petals.

Smiler went under and down and down until he thought it would go on for ever. Then, slowly, the motion stopped and he began to kick for the surface, his nose and mouth full of water where his hand had been jerked away from his nostrils. He kicked upwards against the weight of the rucksack and, when he thought it would never happen and he would burst from holding his breath, he was on the surface. For a moment he rode there, swinging high and low on the wave troughs, panting and fighting for breath. From the corner of his eye he saw Dobby's rock. A quick glance upwards showed him that the cliff top held no watcher. He swam towards the cliff well to the right of the rock. He knew exactly where the underwater arch was in relation to the rock. It was hard work with the silver-weighted rucksack dragging at his back and the mad turmoil of water at the cliff foot tossing him here and there, but after a little while he judged that he was in the right position.

He trod water for a moment and took a deep breath. Then, with all the strength he could muster, he heaved himself up and porpoise-dived down, fighting with arms and legs to get low enough to go through the archway and saying to himself, Keep going, Samuel M. Keep going. . . .

Two minutes later Bacon arrived at the cliff top and began to run to and fro along its length, barking and whining. A little while after that Billy Morgan and the Chief Mate arrived. Billy Morgan, no fool, had heard Bacon barking in the room when they had lost Smiler in the castle. He had let the dog out and the two men had followed it through the castle maze and finally out on to the battlements at the back. Here Bacon had jumped down the wall and raced away through the pines after Smiler. The two men had gone back through the castle and had followed up through the pines as fast as they could.

They stood now looking along the line of the cliffs and watching Bacon racing up and down and barking.

Through the wind the Chief Mate said, "What you think, Billy? Is he makin' a swim for it?"

Billy turned on him with a snarl. "You fool. Look at the water. No one would try that. Take a header down there and try to get across to the shore? What you think the boy is? Superman?"

"Then where is he?"

"Hidin' along these cliffs somewhere. He knows the place well. He's here somewhere and we're going to find 'im – and when we do I'll welt the skin off his rear end good and proper. He probably knows some cave or nooky place. We'll find it. But we ain't taking no chances. He might have doubled back and be trying for the boats."

"Well, he can't use ours," said the Chief Mate. "I got the spark plug in me pocket."

"Maybe – but he might be mad enough to try the other boat. He ain't wantin' in guts. You get back there and make sure he can't use it – and keep your eyes peeled. You see 'im – then give him a touch of lead around his legs. That'll bring him up short. I'll see what I can do with the tike."

The Chief Mate began to trot off along the cliff top towards the jetty with the gun under his arm. Billy Morgan started to search along the rocks and boulders that reached a little way down the cliffs.

Bacon, who had lost the scent of his master, went with him, his barking now changed to a low, anxious whining.

Billy Morgan was a methodical man, especially when he wanted something badly. And right now he wanted Smiler and the silver and jewels. He made a careful examination of the cliff top as far as the westerly point, the wind buffeting at him and the rain squalls drenching him. Then he came back and worked the cliffs all the way up until the point where they began to slope down to the little promontory that sheltered the castle bay. Here he was met by the Chief Mate, who reported that he had fixed the boats so that Smiler couldn't use them.

"No sign of 'im?" he asked Billy Morgan.

"No. But the young devil's around somewhere."

"What we goin' to do, then?"

Billy Morgan rubbed his fat chin thoughtfully and then said, "I'm goin' back to where the dog was and do some serious thinkin'."

The Chief Mate's eyes widened. "What, in all this weather?"

"If it snowed enough to put out the fires of Dingley Dell, I wouldn't leave this cliff while there's a scrap of daylight. That silver and tom-foolery is ours and I means to 'ave it. Now you get back to the castle kitchen and fetch up some food. I'm going to find that lad. Nobody hands Billy Morgan one in the bread-basket and gets away with it."

* * *

In the underwater cave Smiler sat on the ledge below the niche in which he had found the Elphinstone jewels. Although there was some light coming in from the thin slit high up in the roof, it was darker in the cave than he had known it before. It was also colder.

Three feet below his ledge the surface of the cave water, taking turbulence from the rollers outside, sloshed and slapped around sending little gouts of spray spurting up on to the ledge.

Smiler had come through the cave entrance all right, but the weight of the heavy, water-sodden rucksack had held him down so that he had had to fight his way to the surface. He flopped over now on his back, exhausted. Trickles of water streamed away over the ledge from his wet clothes and the water-logged rucksack.

For about five minutes Smiler lay flat out, getting his strength and his breath back. Then he slowly sat up and began to take stock of his position. Above the noise of the water in the cave he could hear the whistle of the wind through the crack high above him. He stood up and stripped off his clothes and wrung all the water he could from them. Then he spread them over the rock face so that they would dry out a bit. It was at this moment that he realized that he was hungry. Remembering that the Skipper had a supply of beer in his rucksack, he wondered if the man had kept food there as well. He pulled out the silver and the jewels and stacked them neatly against the rock wall. At the bottom of the rucksack were two cans of beer, a large unopened bar of chocolate, and a packet of biscuits wrapped in cellophane through which the water had not penetrated.

Smiler had a breakfast of a small piece of chocolate,

three biscuits, and a can of beer. He was careful about not eating too much food, but he had no worry about getting thirsty because he could always drink the loch water.

Sitting there, as naked as the day he was born, and finding the hard rock unkind on his bare bottom, Smiler began to sort things out.

Thing Number One was that at the moment he was safe and he had the silver and jewels. In two or three days, he knew, Laura and the Laird would be up. All he had to do was to sit things out until then. . . . At least, he thought that was all. But when he began to think about that, then Thing Number Two came popping into his mind. In those two or three days the Skipper and the Chief Mate wouldn't be idle. They would be looking for him. They would know he was hiding somewhere because they would know that he could never have swum from the island to the loch shore in this weather with a thumping heavy rucksack on his back. For certain they would make a thorough search of the island – and they wouldn't be the only searchers. The moment they let Bacon out of the bedroom (might already have done so), then Bacon would come looking for him. And Bacon had a good nose and would certainly lead them to the cliffs. Holy Crikeys, he thought – Bacon could spoil everything! First thing you'll know, Samuel M., he told himself, is that that old Bacon will be sniffing away at that cliff crack up there and then barking his head off if he gets a scent of you. . . . It mightn't happen right away but sooner or later it would. And when it did, all the Skipper and the Chief Mate would want would be a pickaxe and crowbar to break their way in from the top.

Sitting cross-legged, munching at his biscuits and sipping his beer, Smiler gave the situation very hard thought. Time, he decided, was not on his side. He had to get help as soon as he could. The moment the Skipper saw anyone coming up to the island he knew the man would run for it – and to bring help to the island while this weather lasted could only be done in one way. Laura would never come up unexpectedly on a friendly visit while the weather was bad. But, if he could somehow get back to the castle when it was dark and hoist the flag to half-mast, then early the next morning someone on the mainland would see it, and maybe see it long before the Skipper noticed it. In fact the Skipper might never notice it. And then – suddenly Smiler felt more cheerful – it wouldn't just be Laura who came up. It would be her father and brother, all anxious to know what the trouble was.

That's it, Samuel M., Smiler told himself, that's it. You got to sneak out tonight and get that flag up to half-mast.

*　　*　　*

While Smiler was in his cave, sorting things out and planning his future movements, the Skipper and the Chief Mate were not idle. Billy Morgan, though he was a rogue and a villain, was far from being an unintelligent man – and his intelligence was spurred now by the thought of losing the wonderful load of swag which he had found in the castle.

So, for the whole of that morning, he searched the cliffs methodically and to help him he had Bacon. He made a rough collar and lead with the cord with which he had bound Smiler's hands, and he worked Bacon slowly along the line of the cliffs and the rocks and boulders and gullies just below their crests before they fell away in sheer rock faces. It was hard work in the high wind and stinging rain but Billy Morgan kept at it until he had searched the whole cliff top again and again and again. Each time Billy Morgan and Bacon passed within a few feet of the cliff crack which let light into Smiler's cave. But the slit was hidden in the crevice of two horizontal overlapping rocks and not visible to any passer-by. If the weather had been clear and windless Bacon would almost certainly have caught the scent of Smiler coming from the cave. But this day there was no hope of his doing so. The wind and rain tore along the brink of the cliffs sweeping all scent away.

In the end Billy Morgan realized that this was probably the reason for Bacon's lack of success. But, if the weather wasn't helping him in his search, he knew that so long as it lasted there was no hope of Smiler getting off the island. And the weather had become worse. The wind had strengthened to almost gale force and it was heavy with rain. Now and again from the surrounding hills there were long, rolling peals of thunder and vicious blue jabs of lightning.

Billy Morgan and the Chief Mate took turns for the rest of that day to stand watch on the length of cliff in case Smiler should come out of his hiding place. They wore old mackintoshes which they had found in the castle storeroom. While one was on watch the other ate, rested and got dry in the castle.

Down at the jetty the two boats had been made secure. The spark plug had been taken from the outboard motor and the oars of the Laird's boat had been carried up to the castle and hidden. In addition, the Chief Mate had found a length of chain and a padlock and key in the storeroom. He had passed the chain round the centre thwart of the Laird's boat and looped it around the centre thwart of their own boat, and then through an iron mooring ring in the jetty wall. Nobody could move the boats without unlocking the padlock or cutting the chain.

It was not until darkness fell that the two men gave up their shared vigil on the clifftop. They retired to the castle for the night where the peat fire in the great hall had been piled high so that they could dry off their wet clothes.

They made themselves comfortable with a glass of the Laird's whisky each before the fire.

The Chief Mate said, "How long we goin' to keep up this lark, Billy?"

Billy Morgan said, "Now don't you start fussin', Chiefy. So long as this weather lasts nobody's comin' up here. And as one what 'as done his time at sea I can tell you that it's set for a couple of days at least. That lad's a-hidin' somewhere with all our tom-foolery from the nicest tickle that ever was. I ain't givin' that up until I have to. That lad's only got a few biscuits and a piece of chocolate and growin' lads have got demandin' Auntie Nellies. If we can't find 'im with the dog – then he'll be out for food sooner than later. He won't come out for nothin' else – so we can both sleep in the kitchen tonight. That's where all the grub is. And we'll 'ave the dogs with us."

"But say we 'ave to give it up?" said the Chief Mate.

"Then we 'as to, Chiefy, and we'll 'ave worked

for over a month for no more than this bit of chicken feed." As he spoke he pulled Smiler's money envelope from his pocket and slipped the notes out on to his knees.

"How much?" asked the Chief Mate.

Billy Morgan counted the notes and said, "Little more than a pony. . . . Hullo, what's this?" From among the notes Billy picked out a piece of folded paper. He spread it open and after a moment or two he said, "Well, well, who'd 'ave believed it? 'Ere, take a dekko at this."

He handed the paper over to the Chief Mate and then leaned back in his chair. Staring at the ceiling he said aloud to himself, "Well, well . . . come the worse and you felt real nasty, Billy . . . then real nasty you could be. . . . Yes, real nasty. . . ." He slowly began to chuckle to himself and it was not a very pleasant sound.

*   *   *

Late that afternoon it had grown so cold in the cave that Smiler had put on his partly dried clothes. To keep himself warm he did some exercises but they did not seem to help much. However, they did make him hungry, and by the time darkness came all his chocolate was gone and half the biscuits.

Once the darkness came, the cave became a very eerie place. The sloshing and slapping of the water filled it with weird echoes and sounds and he could see nothing at all.

He lay down on the uncomfortable ledge and shut his eyes and set himself to wait. But the trouble was that he had no idea of how much time was passing.

Smiler didn't like the situation at all. It was like being buried alive and he could understand how it would be very easy to let himself go and get panicky. Being a sensible sort, he decided that he must do something about it, so he started to think of all the things that had happened to him since he had run away from approved school . . . all the nice things and the bad things and all the nice people and the bad people – like the Skipper. With his eyes shut he went through the whole history and, to his surprise, he found that it helped him a lot. He thought about Laura and the Laird, and then his father and the *Kentucky Master* – the first of October wasn't far off now – and then of Laggy. Where was Laggy now, he wondered. And then it struck him that out of something bad, like the Skipper firing at the greylag, something good had come. That was a real tickler, good coming out of bad. . . .

So Smiler passed the time until he thought it was sufficiently late for him to make his foray. Stiff from lying on the ledge, he got up and stripped off all his clothes except his underpants. He had decided that once he was outside the cave he would swim westwards along the cliff. It was not so far that way before he could get ashore. To try and swim eastwards up the loch, along the line of cliffs and round the bay was much farther. Moreover, it would take him against the loch current.

Feeling his way cautiously, Smiler dropped over the ledge into the shallow water and then launched himself gently outwards. He swam by guesswork until his hands felt the wet rock above the cave entrance. Backing a little, he took a deep breath and dived down, hands and arms outstretched to find the side of the cliff opening. To his surprise as he went deep he saw the opening at once as a grey wavering outline lit by the faint light of the night outside. He swam through and surfaced without trouble. He trod water for a few moments. After the darkness of the cave, he was able to see quite easily the line of cliffs and the white crests of the breaking waves. But when he started to swim westwards he realized that it could not be done. Something had happened to the set of the loch current. Instead of running east to west along the cliffs, it was now setting strongly from west to east. Smiler turned and went with it on the longer, but now easier, haul up and round into the bay. As he swam he worked out that the bad weather from the west and the driving wind must have altered the loch current.

Once outside the cave and being taken easily along the cliffs, although the water was rough, Smiler felt much happier. He was a strong swimmer and the long rollers did not worry him, and it was nice to be doing something instead of stuck in that cave getting a sore bottom on the rocks.

Ten minutes later Smiler reached the steps of the jetty. He lay half in and half out of the water, looking at the two moored boats and then up to the dim silhouette of the castle against the dark, clouded night sky. The wind was still very strong, but for the time being there was no rain.

Smiler went up the steps and examined the boats. He saw at once the padlock and chain and made a face to himself. The Skipper was no fool. From the top of the jetty Smiler went away to the right, keeping just along the fringe of the beach, and then circled away to the flight of steps that led up on to the battlements at the righthand side of the castle where the flag-hoist was. The flag was always kept there, attached to the halyard and rolled-up ready to be broken free by its retaining lanyard. If the Skipper knew about the flag signals and had taken the flag away – then he was sunk.

But the flag was there. Smiler freed the halyard from its cleat and hauled the flag up the long face of the corner tower and then on to the tall flagpole that rose from the tower roof. Looking up it was difficult to see how far the rolled flag had gone. When he thought it was about far enough he broke it with a tug on the other halyard haul and at once he saw the whiteness of the Saint Andrew's cross stream pale and ghostly into the wind. The flag was too far up the pole so he lowered it to half-mast, fastened the halyards round the cleat, and slipped away down the battlement steps.

Deciding to make a wide half circle around the north side of the island to reach the westerly end of the cliffs, Smiler started across the meadow. He had only gone about fifty yards when a large shape loomed up through the darkness and Mrs. Brown gave a low call. She moved up to Smiler and, lowering her head, sniffed at his bare knees. It was then that Smiler realized that she had not been milked that day. For a moment he was tempted to leave the cow. But then he thought that she might not get milked for a couple of days more if chances went against him. Knowing this would distress the animal he decided to milk her. He went down on his knees and began to strip Mrs. Brown. The cow stood placidly in the gloom chewing the cud. The smell of the warm milk going to waste on the grass made Smiler's mouth water, so – as he milked – he twisted first one teat and then another sideways and squirted the milk towards his mouth. But for as much as he managed to catch in his mouth, four times more just squirted against his face and ran down over his naked shoulders and chest. The thought of how funny he must look made Smiler giggle with the result that he swallowed milk the wrong way and had a choking fit which he had to stifle in case anyone should hear.

Half an hour after Smiler had finished milking Mrs. Brown he was back in his underwater cave. Somehow now the total darkness did not seem so unfriendly or frightening, nor did the cave feel so cold. He put on his damp clothes, made a pillow of the rucksack and lay down to sleep.

Five minutes later he sat up suddenly, the skin at the back of his head creeping with fright. A wet hand had passed across his face!

Frozen into immobility by fright Smiler sat bolt upright. To his left the water of the cave splashed and gurgled. Then distinctly near his feet he heard something move, first a scraping, scratching sound and then a quick *flap*, *flap*. The next minute something cold and wet slid along his bare leg.

Smiler let out a yelp and reached down with his hand to push it away. His fingers came into contact with wet fur and there was a little snuffle of pleasure as a whiskery nose was pushed into the palm of his hand.

Smiler almost collapsed with relief. It was Dobby. The animal must have scented him on the island and, unseen, had followed him into the water on his swim back to the cave.

Smiler lay back on his pillow, his heart still bumping from the shock. A little way away he could hear Dobby moving around. Then there was a steady crunching sound which told him that the otter had caught a finnoch or trout and was eating it.

When Smiler woke the next morning, Dobby was gone. Daylight was angling through the roof crack and the cave water itself was shot with swirling gleams of light from outside. By Smiler's side were the bones and scales of the finnoch which Dobby had eaten. Alongside of it was another finnoch, quite a big one, from which a bite had been taken in one flank. Cheered by the light in the cave, Smiler looked at the finnoch and thought, Well, Samuel M., if it comes to it and you can't get any other food then you'll have to try raw fish. Then, standing up, he dived into the green cave pool and had his morning bath.

↶ *The Empty Boat* ↶

The reason that there was more light in Smiler's cave was because the sun was shining from a cloudless sky. But it was no friendly, warm sky. All around the sun was a pale halo of greyish-green light, and the westerly wind had moved a few points to the south and was blowing even harder than the day before. It was the kind of weather which at one glance would have made any fisherman decide that it was time to do a little net mending and stay in harbour.

The wind was blowing full gale force now and great waves were breaking over the westerly point of the island, thundering against the rocks and sending spouting cascades of water halfway up the cliffs. Driven in from the sea and circling over the eastern end of the loch were clouds of gulls, terns and other seabirds, wheeling and dipping in the wind. The cairns and rocky ledges of the Hen and Chickens were covered with the roosting birds, all squared round with their heads pointing down wind.

Billy Morgan and the Chief Mate were astir at first light. The Chief Mate made breakfast for them both and, because he was a somewhat more considerate man than his boss, he made up plates of scrap for Bacon and Midas.

After breakfast Billy Morgan and the Chief Mate made a thorough search of the island, beating through all the bushes and likely hiding places, and even examining the swaying, wind-tossed tops of the pines and ashes. They took Bacon with them on the lead, but Bacon showed no interest in their search until they reached the cliff top again. Then Bacon began to whine and bark and Billy Morgan let him off the lead. Bacon immediately ran to the point on the cliff from which Smiler had jumped into the water.

Watching him Billy Morgan said, "Either that tike is a damned fool or he knows something we don't know. There's nothing for it, Chiefy, but to give them there cliffs one more good going over."

"Goin' over," said the Chief Mate gloomily, "is just what will happen if you gets too near in this wind. I reckon we leaves it for a few hours. Maybe the wind'll drop as the sun gets higher."

"Blow harder more likely," said Billy Morgan. But since he no more relished being blown off the cliff top than the Chief Mate did, he agreed to wait for a few hours. They both went back to the castle, leaving Bacon racing up and down the cliff top in his own search for Smiler.

Two things so far neither of the men had noticed. One was the big white stain in the meadow grass where Mrs. Brown had been milked. And the other was the flag of Saint Andrew which streamed in the wind at half-mast.

During the morning Smiler finished the last of his biscuits and was down to drinking the loch water. From the fierce whistling of the wind across the cliff crack and the increased agitation of the water inside the cave he knew that the weather outside must be blowing very hard, harder in fact than the day before because the wind-note from the slit above him was much higher and fiercer. The waves on the loch outside

185

would be far too big to risk a rowing boat, he knew. Even if, Samuel M., he told himself, there was a boat to be got. It would need a stout hacksaw to cut through the chain that secured the boats.

That day passed slowly for Smiler and for the two men. The wind blew fiercely all day and was far too strong for the two men to risk a close examination of the cliffs. Just after mid-day Bacon gave up his search and came back to the castle. But in the evening, a couple of hours before darkness, there was a sudden lull in the weather. The wind dropped completely and the flag of distress flopped limply against its pole so that there was even less chance of its being seen by the two men or anyone from the loch shore.

From the castle terrace Billy Morgan cast an eye at the sky and the racing waves of the loch outside the bay and said to the Chief Mate, "I ain't spent more years than I like to remember at sea to be fooled by this. I seen the weather play this kind of trick before. This 'ere lull might last an hour, might last six hours. But it'll blow again and next time harder than ever. Come on – we'll 'ave another look at them cliffs."

"What if we don't 'ave no luck, Billy?"

Billy Morgan pursed up his fat face and scratched the little wings of hair alongside his bald head. Then he shrugged his shoulders and said, "Then we must give the lad best and up sticks. We can't risk another day out here. It'll grieve me jam-tart for the rest of me life – but there it is. All that lovely silver and tom-foolery what could 'ave put us on easy street for the rest of our natural – whipped from under our noses. You go and get that dog. If there's any scent up there maybe he'll get it now the wind's gone. That lad's up there in some cave or cranny or my name ain't Billy Morgan."

So Bacon was fetched on the lead and in the windless lull the two men went to the cliff top and freed him. And Bacon found Smiler. With no strong wind to dissipate Smiler's body odour as it came out of the cliff crack when Bacon came to the two over-lapping rocks he picked it up at once. He barked loudly and began to scrape at the rocks and at the loose soil around them. Billy Morgan climbed down to the rocks and leaned out over the top one and saw the long narrow line of the open slit.

Tugging Bacon back to the cliff top he stood in front of the Chief Mate and gave him a big wink.

"We got him," he said. "Dogs always knows. Come on. We got things to get. His scent's comin' out of a crack between two boulders. Could be a cave down there – not that he could 'ave got through the crack. Aye, that's it – must be some underwater entrance. He jumped over and dived in. 'Andy little blighter, ain't he? Yes . . . it's got to be like that or my name ain't Billy Morgan."

"You think so, Billy? Sounds a bit –"

"Course I thinks so – because this 'ere tike tells me so."

*　　*　　*

Sitting inside the cave Smiler was well aware that the wind had dropped. The water still rolled and splashed beneath the ledge, but there was no longer any whistling wind noise from the thin crack high above him. All his clothes had more or less dried out now and he was fully dressed.

187

The going of the wind gave Smiler hope. If the bad weather was going to pass then the heavy seas on the loch would drop within a few hours. Or, at least, drop enough to make it safe for a rowing boat.

"But how, Samuel M.," he asked himself, "do you get the rowing boat?"

He sat there tackling the problem. The oars had for sure been taken away and hidden, but that didn't worry him. Piled at the far end of the jetty were some lengths of timber and planking which had been delivered months before for the construction of new pen houses. With a short piece of planking for a paddle he knew that he would be able to manage the boat. He would go with the current up the loch and edge into the nearest shore. Once on the lochside he could take to the hills. If he had anything like a start, the two men would have no chance of catching him and taking the rucksack from him.

But how did he free the boat? There was a hacksaw in the castle workshop, but the chain was a good stout one. It would take a very long time to cut through it – and a hacksaw at work made quite a lot of noise . . . too much. One of the men, especially if there were no wind to drown the sound, would be bound to hear. How, he asked himself, could he free the boat from the chain? He sat there puzzling about it and then remembered something his father used to say when faced with a tricky problem – "There's more ways than one, Samuel M., of cracking a nut when there's no nut-crackers handy."

Well, thought Smiler, so there might be. You could take a hammer to it, and if you didn't have a hammer –

At this point he jerked upright and smacked

himself on the forehead. "Of course! Of course, you fool, Samuel M.," he told himself out loud. He knew exactly how to do it and to do it fast and with the minimum of noise.

Just then over the wave sounds in the cave he heard a dog bark. He jerked his head up towards the cliff crack. The bark came again and with it this time there was a scrabbling, scraping sound. A small trickle of earth and fine shale cascaded thinly down the inside of the cave on to the ledge. The dog barked again and Smiler knew that it was Bacon. Bacon was up there on the cliffs and had scented him through the crack. Alarmed, he stood up and moved away out of the line of the crack. Pressed against the far wall of the ledge, where he could not be seen by anyone looking through the crack, he waited.

Bacon barked once more, and then the scrabbling sounds ceased. Smiler waited and the minutes passed. No sounds came from the slit. Smiler waited on, but still nothing more was heard. Slowly Smiler relaxed. Maybe Bacon hadn't scented him. Maybe he was just hunting along the cliff and had barked and scratched at the crack out of curiosity. His alarm passed from him and he went back along the ledge, elated by the bright idea he had had about the boat, and began to pack up the rucksack. As soon as it was dark enough he was going to leave.

As time passed the inside of the cave grew darker. The sun dropping to the west threw the outside water into dark shadows and the light from the crack was so faint now that he could hardly see it. Then suddenly Smiler heard Bacon barking once more. Almost immediately there was a heavy *clunk*, *clunk* over his head and then the sharp ring of metal striking stone. A cascade of loose roof debris and earth from around the inside of the crack spilled down the steep cave wall to the ledge. Clearly from outside he heard the sound of men's voices.

Smiler was swamped with a feeling of gloom. They'd found him – and Bacon had been the cause of it all! Pressed against the cave wall out of the sight line from the crack, Smiler heard the thumping and metallic sounds begin again. More thin spills of rubble began to fan down the cave side. He knew exactly what was happening up there. The Skipper and the Chief Mate were attacking the rocks with crowbar and pickaxe. If he took to the water now they would see him and they would only have to get their boat and pick him up. But it was just a matter of time before they broke through the cave roof. How long? If it took them until dark then he might have a chance.

The digging noises stopped. There was silence except for the splashing of the cave water. Suddenly very clear and setting up weird echoes in the cave, a voice came down through the crack.

"All right, me old cock sparrer – we knows you're there. Just you stand well clear of this 'ere 'ole – otherwise you're likely to get a rock on your noggin."

It was the Skipper's voice. Smiler said nothing. They couldn't be sure he was here and he wasn't going to give them any hope.

"Don't feel like speaking, eh? Never mind – we knows you're there. Your old tike told us so."

At this moment a thin torchlight beam suddenly angled down from the crack. It hit the dusty resting ledge six feet away from Smiler, who was pressed back against the cave wall in such a position that no light from the crack could reach him. The light above moved a little, but it had a limited range because of the narrowness of the crack. As it moved Smiler's heart suddenly sank inside him. Shining brightly in the now steady beam was one of the beer cans resting on the ledge where he had been sitting!

The torch clicked off and the Skipper's voice came booming down. "Lost your tongue, 'ave you? Well, well, matey, I hopes as 'ow you enjoyed the beer. But by now your Auntie Nellie must be pretty empty!"

The sound of pickaxe and crowbar started again above Smiler. There was nothing he could do but wait – wait impatiently until it was dark enough for him to risk moving out of the cave. It was all a question now of how long it would take the two men to break into the cave from above. Huddled against the cave wall Smiler told himself that the moment they did, even if it was light still, he was going to take a header into the water for the cave entrance.

*   *   *

While Billy Morgan and the Chief Mate laboured on the clifftop in the fast fading light, sending rocks and boulders tumbling over the cliffside to make an entrance, Laura was working in the kitchen of the Mackay farm at the western end of the loch. She had the television on and was watching it while she did some ironing. She was all alone in the house. Her brother had gone off to spend the evening at his girl friend's house at Lochailort, and her mother and father had motored into Mallaig to visit friends for the evening.

The light in the kitchen was going but she did not switch on the lamps because there was enough glow from the television set to see to do the ironing. As she worked she was thinking about Smiler up at the castle and how he had discovered the Elphinstone jewels and of something that her father had said when she had told the family about it.

"The Laird will give the lad a good reward, that is for certain. Let's hope he makes something of it."

"And why should he not?" Laura had asked stoutly.

"Well, lass, I don't know. But I get the feeling that there's aye something a wee bit wrong with that lad. Turning up from nowhere and no sign of any kith or kin worrying about him. And don't give me that saucy stubborn look of yours just because you fancy the colour of his bonnie blue eyes." The whole family had laughed and Laura had been unable to stop her blushes. Just for a moment she had wished she could have told them the truth about Sammy. Well, one day they would know.

Just then the telephone rang. She went through to the hall to answer it. It was a keeper called Angus Bain who lived over in the next valley south of the loch.

"Is your father there, Laura?"

"No, he's away with Mother to Mallaig for the evening. There's only me here. Can I help ye?"

"Well, I thought ye ought to know. I was up on the tops a wee while back getting an old ewe of mine out of a peat hag she was stuck in. This'll make the third time in a month – the beast is for ever in some trouble. There's one spot up there I can just get a sight of the Laird's place so I took a look through my glasses. My, but there's a fair wave going on the loch just now –"

Suddenly apprehensive, Laura said sharply, "Angus Bain, what are you trying to say?"

"Well, I thought your father ought to know seein' as he acts for the Laird. Is he no away to London, did I hear? That's why I asked myself why should his flag be flying at the half-mast if he's no up there? So, I thought your father ought to know –"

"Thank you, Angus. I'll take care of it. Thank you." Laura cut him off and put down the telephone.

Her heart beating fast, she ran back into the kitchen, switched off the set and her iron, and then began to collect her oilskins. There had been no hesitation in her at all at what she must do. Sammy was up there all alone and the flag was at half-mast.

A few minutes later she was down on the farm quay wearing gum boots, oilskin coat and hat. Behind her in the house she had left a note for her father. She filled up the outboard motor tank with petrol and as she did so cast a look up the loch. The light was almost gone. There was no wind going, but the whole of the loch was seething with long curling rollers setting eastwards towards the castle island. Usually the trip took about an hour, but with the set of waves and the current now with her, she guessed she could do it faster this evening.

She spun the motor into life with the starting cord and swung away from the little stone quay. Once she was well out she realized that it was not going to be an easy trip. She had to regulate her speed so that the following rollers kept sweeping gently under the boat and not breaking over the stern. If she went too fast she took the crests of the rollers and plunged down into the troughs ahead, the bows dipping dangerously low and shipping water. More hurry, less speed, she told herself sensibly and settled down to navigate with care. But for all her care there were times when she could not avoid the boat taking water. Before she was far up the loch she had to have the baler out to keep the level of the water down. As she began to bale, the night came down and the wind returned.

There was still no cloud and she could see well enough. But it was as though all the elements were now conspiring to stop her from getting to the island. The wind which had been a little south of west when it had died away now came back stronger than ever – and from due south. It came up in a shrieking, buffeting mass. It surged up over the heights of the loch south shore and then, full of turbulence from the barrier of the hills, howled down on to the loch in a confusion of air currents that fought and tangled with one another. One moment the wind was ahead, then astern, and then it came sweeping across her starboard beam making the boat yaw away. Within five minutes the long, rolling eastward set of the waves was gone and Laura found herself in a confused, heavy chop of waters that spouted high, now against the bows, now over the stern and then smashing into the sides of the boat.

Although she was frightened, she kept her head. She swung the boat over to the south side of the loch hoping to find calmer water there. If anything it was worse because there was more air turbulence right under the lee of the hills. She veered away to the north side of the loch and found the conditions there almost as bad. The force of the wind was so strong at times that it flattened the high tops of the angry waves and sometimes brought the boat up dead. Her left hand and arm stiff and sore from holding the tiller, Laura baled away at the water in the boat with her right hand. Since she knew there was a fair chance of the boat capsizing she kicked off her gum boots so that if she had to swim they would not hold her down.

The curious thing was that, while she was frightened for herself, working the boat and baling mechanically, her real thoughts were always on the flag at half-mast and there was a misery in her that something had happened to Sammy. Not once did it occur to her to run the boat ashore and seek the haven of the lochside for her own safety. But in the end she was forced to do this because the level of the water shipped aboard began to rise faster than she could bale it out. With the boat sitting heavily and dangerously low in the water she sensibly worked into the north shore. She ran the boat up on to a spur of sand and, although the waves beat at the stern and slewed the boat sideways, she stood up to her thighs in water and baled until it was safe enough for her to take to the loch again. In the next two hours she did this three times. The exhaustion and fatigue made her body ache all over, but not once did she think of giving up. Always she had before her the picture of Sammy in trouble at the castle, lying there maybe dangerously injured or ill. . . .

It was midnight when Laura at last rounded the point of the castle bay. The wind was still blowing strongly from the south but had dropped a little in the last ten minutes. She ran into the jetty and jumped out and tied up. There were no other boats at the jetty.

She raced up to the castle and was met by Bacon, who barked a furious welcome. In the great hall Midas was asleep by the fire and made no move. Shouting his name Laura hurried up the stairs to Smiler's room. The room was empty. She went all round the castle, in a fever of anxiety, looking for him. She searched all the castle with Bacon at her heels and then she took a torch from the kitchen and went through all the animal pens, the wild-fowl enclosure, and then through the woods behind the castle and finally out on to the cliff top. Here, Bacon suddenly raced ahead and led her to a great gaping hole in the side of the cliff where two heavy slabs of rock had been prised away.

Laura leaned over the edge of the hole and shone her torch downwards. She saw the narrow ledge below and the heaving pool of cave water and she knew that this must be the place where Sammy had found the Elphinstone jewels. But there was no sign of Smiler there. On the ledge an empty beer can winked in the beam of her light.

Exhausted and despairing Laura went wearily back to the castle and into the great hall. On the table where she had not noticed it before was a piece of red cloth which she at once recognized as the wrapping from the Elphinstone jewels.

She ran across to the Laird's study and looked in. Her heart sank as she saw the open door of the safe and knew that the silver and the jewels were no longer there.

She went back into the hall and collapsed into the wing-backed chair and oddly into her mind came her father's voice, saying, ". . . but I get the feeling that there's aye something a wee bit wrong with that lad." Almost immediately she was furious with herself for thinking, even for a moment, that Sammy might have taken the jewels on his own account.

Shivering and feeling sick with fatigue and apprehension, she dragged herself into the kitchen and made herself a cup of coffee. Before she had half drunk it she rested her head and arms on the kitchen table and sank into a deep sleep. Against the fatigue and strain of the loch journey, and her worry and fears for Sammy, and the shock of the missing silver and jewels, her mind and body had no defence except a relapse into sleep.

When Laura awoke it was still dark. Putting on her oilskins she went up to the great hall and out on to the terrace. The wind was still blowing a full gale from the south and with it now came solid sheets of rain. The terrace was awash and every spout and gutter of the castle was noisy with the rush of rain-water. Using her torch Laura made another inspection of the surroundings of the castle, but in her heart she knew that she was wasting her time. If Sammy had been on the island she was sure that she would have found him by now. Always at the back of her mind was the thought of the Laird's rowing boat which was missing from its jetty moorings.

She came back and searched the castle once more and then, as the dawn came up, though it brought no cessation of the gale and the rain, she made another inspection of the island. Coming back she saw that there was no food or water for the animals in their pens and one look at Mrs. Brown told her that the cow had not been milked for more than twenty-four hours. To give herself something to do which would take her mind off her thoughts, she watered and fed the animals and then milked Mrs. Brown. Wherever she went Bacon went with her, full of restlessness and whining to himself now and then.

When the daylight had strengthened more she went down through the driving rain and wind to make sure that her boat was still safely moored at the jetty. It was filling with water from the rain and the wave spray that burst over it. She went aboard and baled it out. As she did so she was wondering what she should do next. With the weather as it was she was in no mood to risk the boat trip back to the farm. Last night's experience had been enough for her. Anyway, her parents would know from her note where she had gone. Looking up she saw the castle flag still flapping stiffly in the wind at half-mast. When she went up she decided she would hoist it right up.

Her eyes coming back from the flag, she looked out across the bay towards the Hen and Chickens. She could only just make them out through the driving veils of rain. Now and again the thicker squalls blotted them out altogether. Then, just at the mouth of the bay, she saw something rising and falling sluggishly in the angry surging and rolling waves. A large roller suddenly took the object and swept it upwards and then burst right over it. In that moment of time Laura caught the flash of black and white paint.

She dropped the baler and snatched the canvas

cover off the outboard motor. It took her some time to start the engine, but fifteen minutes later she was motoring across the choppy bay and ran alongside the object. It was the Laird's rowing boat, floating the right side up – but filled to the gunwales with water. The boat was empty and one side of the centre thwart had been smashed clean in half. She circled round it and then headed back for the jetty. As she went her eyes were blinded more by tears than rain and she was praying to herself that Sammy had never been fool enough – no matter what the reason – to risk putting off in the boat while the gale had been blowing. The moment he was outside the bay he would have been helpless.

*　　*　　*

But this was exactly what Smiler had done because he had been given no choice. He had clung to the security of the cave while the Skipper and the Chief Mate had worked at enlarging the hole in the roof. It had taken them a long time and while they had worked the darkness had fallen and the gale had come back, stronger than ever, from the south.

In the end Smiler had hoisted on the heavy rucksack and taken to the water. He had dived out through the entrance. Clinging as close as the breaking waves would allow him to the foot of the cliffs he had swum along them towards the bay, helped by the strong current that still set that way.

Ten minutes after he had gone, Billy Morgan had widened the hole in the cliff enough to allow him to get his head and shoulders through and shine the torch around the cave. It had been empty.

Billy Morgan and the Chief Mate had run up to the jetty to check the boats. They had found the rowing boat gone and the fastening loop of the chain hanging still intact over the side of their own boat.

It was at this moment that Smiler in the rowing boat, half a mile eastward down the loch, had run into disaster. The short plank length he was using for an oar was completely useless and he was drifting helplessly in the wild sea. A wave had taken the boat beam side on, swung it high and capsized it. Smiler, heavy rucksack still on his back, had been thrown into the loch. The boat had rolled right over above him and the keel had struck him on the forehead. He had gone down conscious only of a blinding pain in his head.

II

✎ *Destination Still Unknown* ✎

The bad weather eased a bit as the morning wore on, and just after ten o'clock Laura's father and her brother arrived at the castle in a stout motor boat which they had borrowed from a neighbour. Both were very relieved to find Laura safe and sound. But that did not stop her from getting a scolding from her father for going off in the boat on her own in such bad weather. However, there was little edge to his scolding because he was so relieved to find her safe.

Laura told them all she knew and took them to see the hole in the cave top and then the Laird's rowing boat which had finally drifted ashore in the bay close to the wild-fowl pens.

The two men hauled the boat out on to the beach and tipped the water from it.

Jock Mackay examined the smashed centre thwart and said reflectively, "Something gave that an almighty crack. . . . Aye, a real smack that got. . . ."

Laura turned away. She couldn't stand the sight of the boat. She might have been happier if she could have known that it was Smiler who had cracked the thwart in half. He had done it with a large rock picked up from the beach in order to slip the chain loop free from the boat.

Jock Mackay turned, put his arm around his daughter, and said, "You'd better be coming back with us, lass. The Laird's due back tomorrow. He phoned late last night. There's nothing to be done up here now. If the lad went overboard in last night's weather then –''

Laura pulled away from him and ran up to the castle, her hands over her face.

As Jock made to move after her, his son stopped him, saying, "Leave her a while, Father . . ."

When they did go up to the castle, they found Laura in the great hall, and it was a Laura who had now recovered her self-composure.

She said, "You two go back and bring the Laird up tomorrow. I'm going to stay here. There's all the animals to be looked after and the place is in a mess. And I can tell by looking round that there's been more than Sammy up here recently. The police should know about it as quick as possible."

"You don't think the lad went off on his own account with the silver and stuff?" asked her father.

"Of course I don't! Sammy's no thief! He must have gone off with it to keep it safe from whoever was here. Clearly someone else has been eating in that kitchen. And why would Sammy use a pickaxe and crowbar to open up the cliff top? The sooner you get back and tell the police about this the better. I'll be all right up here. And what's more, I don't think . . . well, I'm sure Sammy's all right somewhere. He's got to be." But although she said it stoutly there was a dark shadow of doubt hovering always at the back of her mind.

Laura's brother said, "Maybe, Father, before we go back we ought to motor round the Hen and Chickens. If the lad put out last night from the bay, the current would take him down that way. If he went overboard he might have made them."

So, before the two men headed west down the loch, they took the boat up to the Hen and Chickens and motored round them all. The strong seas were smashing against their low rock sides and sweeping up their small beaches. Nothing grew on them except some small patches of heather, some sea-holly, and tufts of pink thrift. While his son managed the tiller Jock Mackay got out his field glasses and scanned each little island as they circled it. But he could see no sign of Smiler. The only life on the islands were the roosting flocks of seabirds.

The two men went twice around all the islets and then turned away and made their way back down the loch.

* * *

But the two men, as men often do, were accepting something as fact on the basis of their own experience. Both knew the loch and they were sure that anyone going overboard in the previous night's weather would have had no chance. If they had gone ashore and searched each islet thoroughly they would have learned better, learned that there is always some odd quirk of fate to upset apparent facts and well-proven experience.

Smiler was on the Hen and alive. In the darkness it was a large underwater rock just off the small beach of the Hen that the craft had struck. Smiler had gone overboard and had been hit by the turning keel. The blow had dazed him so much that he did not know what he was doing or what was happening to him. He had gone down and then been sucked up by the maelstrom of waves and thrown towards the beach. When his hands had felt rocks and shingle he had instinctively grappled for a hold. Like some blind, unknowing animal he had crawled forward. A wave had sucked him back from his hold and then another had thrown him forward to the beach. On his hands and knees, bowed down by the weight of the rucksack, he had struggled forward and finally had escaped the reach of the waves. Not knowing what he was doing he had crawled on, panting and sobbing, with nothing to guide him except his powerful instinct to get away from the water.

He lay now, exposed to the searing wind and rain squalls, in a small hollow at the top of the Hen, a hollow that was ringed with weather-worn and bird-marked rocks. On the rocks at this moment was roosting a small flock of black-headed gulls. The birds surrounded Smiler in a silent colony, heads facing the wind, their plumage tightly bedded down to take the air-slip over their bodies. Smiler lay on his face, the rucksack still on his back, and two gulls were perched on the rucksack. It was not surprising that Jock Mackay had not spotted him. From the loch all that could be seen was a flock of gulls sheltering on the rocks.

There was a large bruise on Smiler's right temple and a cut on his left cheek which had ceased bleeding though the rain still kept the wound open and raw. Smiler, after long hours of unconsciousness, was now sleeping and dreaming. In his dream he was out on a sunlit, cloud-shadowed autumn loch in a boat fishing while Laura lazed in the stern with her back to a silent outboard motor. He was playing a sea-trout, the taut line singing from the reel, when from behind him he heard the *thud, thud* of a heavy motor boat engine. He looked round but there was nothing behind him except Laura, her hair teased by the wind, her brown face smiling at him, and a wide stretch of empty water.

It was at this moment, as Jock Mackay's boat was two hundred yards away, heading down the loch, that Smiler opened his eyes and rolled over to his side and groaned. Immediately the flock of gulls went up from around him in a wild, white explosion, calling and screaming in fright.

Slowly Smiler sat up and blinked his eyes to clear them. Rain and wind swept into his face blinding him for a moment. Then the squall passed and he saw the dark shape of the motor boat on the heaving, steely waters moving fast away down the loch. To his ears came the regular *thud*, *thud* of the motor which he had known in his dream.

Smiler flexed his arms and became aware of the heavy rucksack on his back. Awkwardly he slipped it off, every muscle in his body stiff and sore, his head throbbing sharply each time he moved it. He looked down at himself and saw that he was wearing just shirt and trousers and was barefooted. A sudden shivering fit passed through him and his body trembled as though it would never stop until he clenched his teeth and flexed his muscles to halt it.

He gave another groan and then tried to remember what had happened. Slowly it all came back to him. He had smashed the centre thwart to free the rowing boat and had gone out into the bay using his plank paddle. He had heard the Skipper and the Chief Mate shouting behind him. As he had reached the limit of the bay and the current and wild sea had taken him eastwards, he had seen a torch dancing on the jetty. Then it had moved, pitching and swaying, out towards him and he had known that the two men were after him. Beyond that he remembered nothing.

Long after Smiler's boat had capsized, the two men had continued their search for him – but the high seas and howling winds had eventually forced them to look to their own safety. Angry and frustrated they had run for the eastern end of the loch and beached their boat for Willy McAufee to take over. By morning they were miles away in the hills heading for Fort William.

With the gulls crying and circling above him Smiler now stood up unsteadily, swaying in the force of the wind. He knew that he was on the Hen. He looked towards the castle away over the angry waters and it was suddenly blotted from his sight by driving rain.

Smiler sat down. Samuel M., he thought, you can't just sit here. You've got to do something. The rain squall cleared and he saw the castle again. This time he noticed that the flag now flew from the top of the mast. That meant that someone had come up during the night. His body shook with a shivering fit again and his head throbbed. He had to do something, had to get off the Hen before he passed out again. The castle disappeared in the rain but the picture of the flag stayed in his mind. Somebody had answered his signal last night. "What you want now, Samuel M.," he said aloud, "is a signal too." He considered this for a while and then, stiffly and awkwardly, began to make his way down from the rock. He knew exactly what he was looking for.

Fifteen minutes later Smiler was on the point of the Hen nearest the castle island. On the beach he had found a six-foot length of bare oak branch which had been washed ashore. He had fastened his shirt to it by the sleeves to make a rough flag. He sat now on the highest rock he could find, naked to the waist in the buffeting wind and rain, holding his flag aloft. Every now and then his body shook with a spasm of shivering. In the end, exhausted from holding the flag aloft against the tearing wind, Smiler searched around and found a crevice into which he could jam the end of the branch. He wedged rocks around it, too, to keep it in position. Then, feeling ill and completely done-in, he could not stop himself from lying down. In a few moments he was gone from the world in sleep.

If the gale had kept up for the rest of that day things might have gone very badly for Smiler. He was in no shape to pass another night on the Hen. But, in mid-afternoon, the rain stopped and the wind eased down to a steady, firm blow. The shirt flag flew steadily above Smiler who lay sleeping, turning and groaning in his dreams.

On the castle island Laura, trying not to think about Smiler but not succeeding, went about her chores. She had fed and watered all the animals during the morning and then had spent some time tidying up in the castle. In the afternoon when the rain stopped and the gale eased she went into the meadow to milk Mrs. Brown.

As she came back she looked out over the loch towards the Hen and Chickens and caught sight of something fluttering. The next moment she had put down her milk pail and was running for the castle.

She got the Laird's field glasses from his study, focussed them on the Hen, and saw the shirt flying from its crooked staff and something huddled under it.

With a great surge of hope welling in her heart, she ran for the jetty and her boat. She started the motor and cast off. Bacon came racing down the jetty and jumped into the boat with her, barking furiously.

As the boat swept out into the bay Laura said aloud, "Please God, let it be him. And if it is –" her jaw firmed angrily "– no matter if Jock Mackay is my father, he'll hear from me about not searching the Hen properly!"

*　　*　　*

When Smiler awoke he saw at once that Laura was in the room. She was sitting at the window, resting one elbow on the sill and looking out. Against the pale evening sky her profile was etched sharply, and a faint breeze through the half open window stirred her long hair. Although he felt weak and drained, he lay contentedly, just looking at her and feeling a warmth in himself grow because she was there. Never in his life had he been more thankful than when he had seen her boat come tossing towards the point of the Hen. When she had rushed up to him and hugged her arms around him he could do no more than just shiver and tremble against her and say her name over and over.

She had brought him back to the castle, seen him to bed, and had wedged him around with three hot water bottles. Then she had brought him hot milk and made him take some aspirins. When he had wanted to talk, she had shaken her head severely. He was asleep within seconds of finishing his milk.

Through the window now he could hear the call

of pigeons and the cry of gulls. An early star showed in the pale oblong of sky and he knew that the wind and rain had gone, that the fierce gale was over. Putting his hand up to his cheek he realized that she had stuck a strip of plaster over his wound while he had slept. His head still ached a little and the bruise on his forehead had come up in a large bump. His body felt as though every muscle had been over-stretched on a rack.

Slowly, sensing that he was awake, Laura turned her head and smiled at him. She got up and came across to the bed. Without a word she knelt down and took his hand. With an instinctive, unthinking movement she leaned forward and rested her cheek against his. Smiler had never known a moment like it before in his life. He had the feeling that not only was he safe for ever, but that he could never be lonely or afraid in his life ever again.

Without a word they stayed like that for a while. Then Laura suddenly stood up and turned away from him so that he could not see her face.

Smiler said, "It's all right, Laura. And I'm all right too." Then, his voice rising, he went on, "And do you know – Laggy flew! When the Skipper fired his gun he just took off. Right across the bay, *flap*, *flap* and up and away down the loch. Holy Crikeys, it was really something to see!"

Laura turned back, her face composed now, and asked, "Who's the Skipper?"

"Oh, I forgot. 'Course you don't know about him. And the Chief Mate."

Laura said with unexpected primness, "There's a lot I don't know – and there's a lot I've got to know. But if you think you're going to tell me it now,

Sammy, you've got another think coming. You don't do or say a thing until you've got some decent food into you."

Smiler gave her a grin and said, "You sound just like a nurse in a hospital."

"Aye, and that's how I mean to sound and be until you're your proper self again. Now, you just rest there until I get ye something."

"I'm starving," said Smiler. "What am I going to have?"

"Wait and see," said Laura as she went to the door.

"That's what my Sister Ethel always used to say."

Half an hour later Laura brought him a bowl of soup and three poached eggs on toast and a dish of tinned fruit.

While he was eating Smiler told her the story of his adventures. Laura sat on the end of the bed and listened with a severe expression on her face. Outside the night darkened and the flames of the four candles in the room wavered gently in the faint draught from the window.

When Smiler had finished Laura said, "I've no idea who the two men could be. They fit no one around these parts. And I'll doubt whether they're hanging around here now. They've taken to their heels. But I can tell ye, if that sly loon Willy McAufee had anything to do with this he's going to be sore sorry for himself."

In fairness Smiler said, "Well, I don't know that he did. Only that the men had a list of the hiding places where the Laird used to keep his key." He slowly grinned at her and said, "Do you know what an Auntie Nellie is?"

"No, I do not."

"Or a troubled-Harold?"

"Sammy Miles, is your mind wandering?"

"No. Auntie Nellie is your belly. And troubled-Harold is a double-barrelled shotgun. That's what the Skipper called them."

"You sound as though you liked the villain."

"No, I did not. But he had a funny way of speaking. He called the jewellery tom-foolery." Then, with a lack of bashfulness which surprised him even as he spoke, Smiler went on, "Can I ask you something very private, Laura?"

"How would I know until you've asked it?"

"Well, it's about the Elphinstone jewels. The Laird's going to be very pleased, isn't he?"

"Aye, he is. But that's no private matter."

"Well, it is in a way. You might get your farm, you know."

"Away with ye. That's just happy talk."

"And he might, when – well, when the bit of trouble I'm in is cleared up – arrange for me to study. You know, to be a vet."

"Aye, he might. But you're a long time getting to the private part."

"I'm coming to it now," said Smiler grinning and still surprised that he felt no awkwardness. "What I want to know is . . . well, when I'm really grown up and a vet . . . well, would you marry me?"

For a moment Laura's face showed her surprise, then she gave a little frown and said severely, "Sammy Miles, that bump on your head has made you lose your wits. You must be daft to think I'd answer a question like that."

Smiler lay back against his pillows and said, "You

don't have to answer it now. But when I get to be a vet – well, you just watch out. I'm jolly well going to come and ask you. I never did meet anyone like you before and just think – if I was a vet and you had a farm –"

"And if pigs had wings they would fly and a fine old world that would be."

Tight-faced Laura came to the bed and took his tray, but as she moved away she turned and smiled back at him and said, "Mind you – if you did come and ask I'd no say that I wouldn't give it serious thought. But for now, you get your head down on those pillows and go to sleep. I'll be up in a little while to snuff your candles."

When Laura had gone, Smiler lay back on his pillows and thought how pretty she looked. Not just when she smiled and laughed, but also when she tried to look stern and cross. She was a wonderful girl. Holy Crikeys, she was. Not like the rest. She could do things that would make most other girls turn and run. . . . Despite the low throbbing still in his head he grinned happily to himself and thought, Samuel M., the sooner you get to be a vet the better.

When Laura came up an hour later he was locked in sound sleep. She leaned over him and arranged the clothes around his shoulders and then slowly put out a finger and touched his sun-tanned, freckled cheek above the cut on his face.

The next morning to Smiler's surprise he found that he felt worse than he had done the previous night. Laura noticed it at once and she took his temperature and checked his pulse. But all she would say when Smiler asked her about them was, "They're aye fair enough. But what you've got is a . . . a sort of reaction. You'll not be getting out of that bed in a hurry, I can tell ye."

But Smiler had no wish to get out of the bed. He slept on and off during the morning and now and again found himself shivering and going cold all over. This was the beginning of a fever that didn't leave him until the following afternoon. During that period things became pretty mixed up for Smiler because he couldn't sort out whether he was dreaming them or whether they were actually happening. Sometimes he was being chased by the Skipper and the Chief Mate all around the island with Bacon barking at his heels. At other times the big four-poster bed seemed to be adrift on a dark, stormy sea. The little carvings on the supporting posts were alive, the flowers and leaves fluttering in the wind, the gnomish men and women clambering up and down, and the red velvet canopy cracking and booming as each gust took it. Once the room was full of deep calm and he saw the Laird and Laura leaning over him. The Laird's face looked grave and he slipped up the sleeve of Smiler's pyjamas and gave him an injection in the arm. As he turned away Smiler saw that he had the small brown owl sitting on his shoulder. The owl twisted its head right round, looked at Smiler, ruffled its feathers, and then gave him a wink from one amber-brown eye.

The curious thing was that when Smiler really did come round the Laird and Laura were standing at his bedside, and the owl was on the Laird's shoulder.

Smiler looked up at them and said, "Hullo."

The Laird smiled and said, "Hullo, Samuel M. How do you feel?"

Smiler said, his mind still a little fogged, "This is

like the first time. The first time I came here. Did I get a drop of malt this time too?"

The Laird laughed. "No – ye got something that worked faster." He reached out and put his hand on Smiler's brow and after a moment nodded. "Twenty-four hours and you'll be your old self. Until then you're under Mistress Laura's orders."

Smiler looked at Laura and met her smile with his own. "She can be very strict, sir."

"Aye, maybe. But ye'll just have to put up with that. . . ." The Laird paused and then put out a hand and ruffled Smiler's fair hair. "This is no time for too much talk, Samuel M. But I'd have you know now that I'm much in your debt. You're a good, brave lad."

Left on his own, feeling weak but much better, Smiler stared at the cloud-flocked patch of blue sky through the window and wondered why it always pleased him so much when the Laird called him "Samuel M." Apart from his father he was the only other one to do so. He had a feeling that in some way it had to have a very special meaning . . . almost as though, while his father was away, the Laird had quite naturally taken his place. Then, thinking about his father, he lay and began to work out in his mind how long it was to the first of October and the return of the *Kentucky Master*. So far as he could make out without a calendar handy he thought it could not be more than just over a week. Well, he would be up and about long before then.

* * *

At that moment in the police station at Fort William,

a sergeant was opening the morning's mail. At the top of the pile was a crumpled white envelope addressed in pencilled block letters and carrying an Edinburgh post-mark.

The sergeant opened it. Inside was a letter on a single sheet of lined writing paper and a newspaper clipping. The letter was written in pencilled block letters and one corner was stained with tea or coffee droppings.

The letter read:

THE LAD WHAT IS MENTIONED IN THE ENCLOSED IS WORKING NOW FOR SIR ALEC ELPHINSTONE AT ELPHINSTONE CASTLE. SENT IN THE NAME OF JUSTICE AND FAIR PLAY. A WELL-WISHER OF THE LAW.

The sergeant picked up the newspaper clipping and began to read it. The clipping, ringed around with red pencil, had been cut from an old number of *The Times*. Actually it had been cut out by Smiler after Sir Alec had shown it to him because he had wanted it to give to his father. He had kept it in his money envelope which Billy Morgan had taken from him.

The sergeant read it through, then read the letter again, and then screwed up his mouth as though he suddenly had a bad taste in it, and said, "A well-wisher of the law, I don't think."

* * *

That day, too, Smiler was allowed up for a couple of hours in the afternoon and he sat in the great hall and told Sir Alec all his adventures, and particularly about the way Laggy had flown off.

The day after that he felt so much better that he was allowed to get up in the morning on the understanding that he took a rest after lunch. During the morning the Laird brought out the Elphinstone jewels and he told Smiler some of their history and he made Laura, who was still at the castle, wear some of them.

As she stood before them with the glowing emeralds around her brown neck and the eight-pointed star on her brow, gleaming under her dark hair, the Laird said, "And don't either of ye think I'm not a man of my word. You'll both get your reward."

Smiler, his eyes on Laura, saw her suddenly blush, and then he knew that he was blushing too and all he wanted to do was to get up and go out on the terrace and hide his face. But before he could move, a familiar stubborn, stern look came over Laura's face. Taking off the jewels, she said primly, "Well, I've no time for fancy parading around all morning. There's work to be done in the kitchen."

When she had gone Smiler and the Laird went for a walk outside and the Laird was full of all the different things he would now be able to do to his properties and in setting up a wild-life sanctuary at this end of the loch.

"We'll have it properly guarded, lad, so no thieving nest robbers can get in. There were ospreys here this spring that had their eggs taken. With luck they'll be back next year and things will be different. And we must not be selfish . . . we'll fix it so that the public can come on certain days and enjoy it too. And you, Samuel M. . . . well, when your bit of trouble is settled, you can get your head down to some real hard work towards becoming a vet. But it will no be easy. You'll be starting late and you've a lot of lee-way to make up. But it can be done if you set your heart on it. Aye, it can be done. . . ."

As they made their tour of inspection, Smiler was full of questions about just how you went about being a vet and the Laird explained to him exactly what would have to be done; the subjects to be studied, the examinations to be taken, and the years of hard work ahead. The awful thought suddenly came to Smiler that if it was going to take all that while – not that he minded the hard work and so on – it might be that by the time he really was a qualified vet Laura might have become married to someone else . . . Holy Crikeys, what a terrible thing that would be!

The Laird, seeing his long face, said, "Are you all right, Samuel M.? You look as though you've lost a shilling and found a penny."

"Oh, I'm all right, sir. Thank you, sir," said Smiler. "I was just wonderin', sir, whether I could do all the studying somewhere here in Scotland? So, well, so that I could come sometimes and see you and . . . well, everyone else?"

The Laird considered this and then said, "Aye, it could be arranged – if your father's agreeable. When he's back and you've cleared up things we'll see about it."

Smiler's heart lifted.

After lunch that day Laura ordered Smiler up to his room to take his rest. With his shoes off he lay on the bed fully clothed, staring out of the window, thinking about the years of work ahead of him and of his father now soon due at Greenock. He was sure that his father would agree to his living in Scotland. Gradually he drifted off into sleep.

He woke an hour later. Although he had promised to stay in the room until Laura called him, he felt too restless to stay and decided to risk her anger. He put on his shoes and went quietly down through the castle and on to the wide landing above the great hall. A beam of sunlight struck through the great mullioned window and lit up the painting of Lady Elphinstone. She was a very grand lady, he thought, but by no means as beautiful as Laura. He turned from the painting and, leaning on the top balustrade, looked down into the hall.

It was at this moment that he realized that there were people in the great hall. Their voices came clearly up to him. He moved along the balustrade, almost to the top of the stairs and crooked his neck to look down.

The Laird was standing to one side of the stone fireplace. Near the long table, their backs to him, Smiler saw two men in uniform. They were policemen. Their hats with checked bands rested on the table. The taller of the two – who was an inspector – was speaking to the Laird, who held two pieces of paper in his hand and was frowning over them.

"They came through the post anonymously, Sir Alec. That kind of thing usually does. But I'm afraid, sir, we have to act on it just the same. I take it you knew this lad's history?"

An awful feeling of emptiness swept through Smiler. He saw the Laird approach the long table and put down the two pieces of paper. Even from where he was he recognized the crumpled newspaper cutting with a large red pencil circle around it.

The Laird said, "Aye, Inspector, I knew. But some things you know and then properly forget. You have your job to do, I know. But there is no doubt in my mind that the lad is innocent. More than that, he is absolutely convinced that when his father docks at Greenock on the *Kentucky Master* in a few days' time . . . well, then as a boy should, he's certain that his father can sort things out for him. And I've no doubt at all that he will."

The Inspector looked at the other policeman, hesitated, and then said, "Sir Alec – we've been some time getting around to this visit here. That's because we've been in touch with the English police authorities. When this lad went on the run again from Wiltshire, the English police felt that his father should be brought home to help deal with the situation. They got in touch with the shipping company who cabled the *Kentucky Master* on which this Mr. Miles was serving as a cook. Unfortunately the father was not on board. It seems that he failed to report back to the ship when it left Montevideo many weeks ago. Nobody knows what has happened to him. I'm afraid the lad has got to go back to the English police and the approved school. Maybe there'll be deeper enquiries into the theft affair in due course, but for the time being that's what must happen to him. I'm sorry, sir, but I must ask you to hand the lad over to us."

"Good God, this will break the lad up completely!" The Laird paced away towards the terrace, pulling hard at his beard.

But Smiler hardly saw him or heard any more of

the talk. What could have happened to his father? A host of black fears invaded his mind.

Swamped with despair he turned blindly away from the balustrade and moved back past the painting of Lady Elphinstone, his head bowed, his shoulders shaking. It was then that he felt someone take his arm gently. He didn't have to look up to know it was Laura who must have come quietly up behind him and overheard the talk.

She put her arm round his shoulders and led him back up the stairs into his room. As she closed the door Smiler turned and she put her arms around him and held him while he fought to master his black sorrow. She held him tight and, shaking, he buried his face in her shoulder. Then, after a little while, he began to control himself. Through all his anguish he knew that he must take a grip on himself.

Suddenly he stepped away from Laura and looked full at her, his face tear-streaked, his mouth set obstinately.

"I'm not going with them! It's all wrong! I'm sure my father's all right. Nothing could have happened to him. And I never ever stole anything! I'm not going with them!" he shouted.

Laura said, "Oh, Sammy . . . Sammy . . . you can't do anything else . . ."

"Yes, I can. If . . . well, if there's no one else to help me, I can help myself. But I'm not going back to that school. Never!"

"Be sensible, Sammy. They'll come after you. They'll –"

"Let them. But they've got to catch me first. No, I'm not going with them."

He turned quickly and went to the wardrobe,

pulling open the door. Before he could take out any clothes Laura was at his side. She slipped between him and the wardrobe.

"Sammy – one last time. Think. You've got to think and be sensible."

Bitterly Smiler said, "If my father's not coming back yet . . . well, then I got to do things for myself. But one thing I'm never going to do is go back to that school. I'm not staying there for something I never did." He put out an arm to ease her aside. "Let me get my things."

Laura held her ground. For a moment or two she looked him squarely in the eyes and then she said quietly, "You're wrong, Sammy. Aye, you're awful wrong. But I can see you must do what you must do. And since you must do it, I'm no the one to stand in your way. You're going to run for it again – is that it?"

"Yes."

"Then I can do no more than help you. Listen, you're supposed to be resting here another hour and the Laird will not let them disturb you until then. Now you go out the back way and meet me on the far side of the water-fowl pens. And don't worry about your things here. I'll see to them." She moved him away from the wardrobe.

"Oh, Laura, thanks. And I know what I'm doing is right."

Laura shook her head. "I doubt it fine. But there was never a woman could make a man see sense when he didn't want to. Now, out with you."

Heavy with a numbing grief, not even trusting himself to think any more of his father than that he was missing, pushing all the memories of them together from him, Smiler left the room and made his way quietly out through the back of the castle.

Fifteen minutes later, hiding in the shade of the trees the other side of the pens, Smiler saw the Laird's black and white row boat slide round a rocky bluff and glide into the shore. Laura was at the oars and there was Billy Morgan's old water-stained rucksack on the floor boards, packed with Smiler's clothes and few possessions.

Without a word Smiler got into the boat and Laura went down the side of the island to keep out of sight of the castle. At the end of the island, as she began to swing the boat out to cross to the loch's north shore, Smiler looked back at the towers of the castle just showing over the tips of the pines. The thought of the Laird there and all the animals knifed through him in a sharp pain. He had planned one day to bring his father there. . . . Had known how his father, who was as mad about animals as he was, would love it. He fought to keep his tears back. He was on his own. He had to be tough. . . .

Laura said, "Bacon wanted to come, but I shut him in my room. You'd no get far with him around. There's most of your things in the rucksack and a bit of money. Where I'm going to land you there's a track up through the woods. At the top of the woods you'll hit an old road. Keep along it and you'll finally make the Fort William road. After that . . ."

Smiler looked across at her. He knew she thought he was doing wrong. But he couldn't help that. He just had to get away, right away, and when things were more settled he would have to work everything out for himself. He only had himself now. . . .

Whatever could have happened to his father? Tears suddenly misted his eyes.

A little later the boat grounded on the shore at the foot of the woods. Laura jumped out and pulled the boat up on to the sand and Smiler followed her with the rucksack.

They stood together in the afternoon sunshine. High up in the blue a pair of golden eagles soared in lazy sweeping circles. Down the shore sandpipers called and a handful of redshanks flickered with white-barred wings over the water.

Smiler put down the rucksack and said brokenly, "Thank you. . . . Thanks, Laura. I hope . . . well, I hope you don't get into trouble over this –"

"Oh, Sammy!" Suddenly Laura put her arms round him and hugged him, kissing his cheek, and then for a moment their lips met. It was a moment Smiler would always remember, her lips against his, her loose hair in his face, and the slow shake of her shoulders under his hands.

The next moment he stepped away from her and picked up the rucksack. Two yards apart they looked at one another, each with tears in their eyes. Then Smiler said, "Goodbye, Laura. Don't worry, I'll be back sometime."

He saw Laura's face go slowly stubborn and set. The look was one he had often seen before, and she said firmly, "You'd better be back sometime, Sammy. You'd just better for I'm not forgetting you've made me a promise to ask a certain question one day. Now, away with you, you daft loon, and keep your eyes skinned for the police – they'll be hoppin' mad about this. And let them be!"

*　　*　　*

Six hours later when the cars moving along the road had turned their sidelights on, Smiler stepped out of the cover of a clump of bushes at the roadside and raised a hand for a lift to a car coming up the road. He did it without much hope because many cars had passed, ignoring his signals.

But this car stopped a few yards past him. It was a very old four-seater touring car with a canvas hood which had been patched in a few places. The paint-work was shabby and the nearside back mudguard had a big dent in it. As Smiler came abreast of it, the driver leaned across and looked out of the near-side window. He was a large-faced, middle-aged man wearing a battered straw boater with a coloured ribbon around it. He had a black, thickly waxed sergeant-major's moustache that curled into sharp points at each end. In his mouth was a pipe with a piece of insulating tape around the broken stem. His dark eyes held a lazy, good humoured twinkle.

He said in a slow, easy voice, "Where you headin' for, me dear?"

Smiler said, "I dunno exactly."

The man chuckled, "Destination unknown. Good as any. Hop in."

Smiler opened the car door. As he did so the man said, "Mind Scampi. You'll have to nurse him on your lap. Dump your rucksack with the rest of the junk in the back."

In the half-light Smiler saw, curled up on the shabby leather seat, a very large Siamese cat. The man reached over and lifted the cat. Then, when Smiler was settled, he dumped the cat on to Smiler's lap. The cat opened one baleful eye at the disturbance and then settled to sleep on Smiler's knees.

As the man drove off, he said casually, "Don't be surprised if I make a smart detour now and then suddenlike – but just at the moment, me dear, I'm not anxious to meet any of the boys in blue. Little matter of an unpaid hotel bill at my last stop. Lovely night, ain't it? Lovely, indeed, after the weather we've had. Lovely night, quiet roads, destinations unknown – what more could a man ask for? Beautiful. Beautiful."

For the first time in many hours, almost the edge of a smile touched Smiler's lips.

*   *   *

POSTSCRIPT: In Smiler's room at Elphinstone castle, Sir Alec was reading a note that had been left for him. It ran:

Dear Sir Alec,

Since my father wont be back yet there are things I got to do for myself. Im sorry leaving without saying good bye, but Laura will explain.

I hope Bacon wont be much trouble till I can come for him.

Yours faithfully,
Samuel Miles

General Editors: Anne and Ian Serraillier

Chinua Achebe Things Fall Apart
Douglas Adams The Hitchhiker's Guide to the Galaxy
Vivien Alcock The Cuckoo Sister; The Monster Garden; The Trial of Anna Cotman
Michael Anthony Green Days by the River
Bernard Ashley High Pavement Blues; Running Scared
J G Ballard Empire of the Sun
Stan Barstow Joby
Nina Bawden The Witch's Daughter; A Handful of Thieves; Carrie's War; The Robbers; Devil by the Sea; Kept in the Dark; The Finding; Keeping Henry
Judy Blume It's Not the End of the World; Tiger Eyes
E R Braithwaite To Sir, With Love
John Branfield The Day I Shot My Dad
F Hodgson Burnett The Secret Garden
Ray Bradbury The Golden Apples of the Sun; The Illustrated Man
Betsy Byars The Midnight Fox
Victor Canning The Runaways; Flight of the Grey Goose
John Christopher The Guardians; Empty World
Gary Crew The Inner Circle
Jane Leslie Conly Racso and the Rats of NIMH
Roald Dahl Danny, The Champion of the World; The Wonderful Story of Henry Sugar; George's Marvellous Medicine; The BFG; The Witches; Boy; Going Solo; Charlie and the Chocolate Factory; Matilda
Andrew Davies Conrad's War
Anita Desai The Village by the Sea
Peter Dickinson The Gift; Annerton Pit; Healer
Berlie Doherty Granny was a Buffer Girl
Gerald Durrell My Family and Other Animals
J M Falkner Moonfleet
Anne Fine The Granny Project
F Scott Fitzgerald The Great Gatsby
Anne Frank The Diary of Anne Frank

Leon Garfield Six Apprentices
Graham Greene The Third Man and The Fallen Idol; Brighton Rock
Marilyn Halvorson Cowboys Don't Cry
Thomas Hardy The Withered Arm and Other Wessex Tales
Rosemary Harris Zed
Rex Harley Troublemaker
L P Hartley The Go-Between
Esther Hautzig The Endless Steppe
Ernest Hemingway The Old Man and the Sea; A Farewell to Arms
Nat Hentoff Does this School have Capital Punishment?
Nigel Hinton Getting Free; Buddy; Buddy's Song
Minfong Ho Rice Without Rain
Anne Holm I Am David
Janni Howker Badger on the Barge; Isaac Campion
Kristin Hunter Soul Brothers and Sister Lou
Barbara Ireson (Editor) In a Class of Their Own
Jennifer Johnston Shadows on Our Skin
Toeckey Jones Go Well, Stay Well
James Joyce A Portrait of the Artist as a Young Man
Geraldine Kaye Comfort Herself; A Breath of Fresh Air
Clive King Me and My Million
Dick King-Smith The Sheep-Pig
Daniel Keyes Flowers for Algernon
Elizabeth Laird Red Sky in the Morning
D H Lawrence The Fox and The Virgin and the Gypsy; Selected Tales
Harper Lee To Kill a Mockingbird
Laurie Lee As I Walked Out One Midsummer Morning
Julius Lester Basketball Game
Ursula Le Guin A Wizard of Earthsea
C Day Lewis The Otterbury Incident
David Line Run for Your Life; Screaming High
Joan Lingard Across the Barricades; Into Exile; The Clearance; The File on Fraulein Berg
Penelope Lively The Ghost of Thomas Kempe
Jack London The Call of the Wild; White Fang
Lois Lowry The Road Ahead; The Woods at the End of Autumn Street

How many have you read?